Brigit had fallen in love with Alexis because he was so vibrant, so attractive, so impetuous, so gentle: when he had kissed her,
that first time, in her kitchen, he had half-
lifted her from her chair and stood above her,
gripping her thin shoulders, daringly, yet
almost brotherly, with a physical compassion she no longer associated with men. How
can people say you are sardonic and flippant
and arrogant, Brigit wanted to protest to
him, burying her face in his neck, hugging
his sides, when you are one of the most...the
most congenial people I have ever met...His
sexual grace, his sexual agility, were far less
astonishing than his simple, frank, unanticipated friendliness. She kissed him and
caressed him and stroked him almost with
a sort of greed, a hunger she hadn't known
was in her....

Fawcett Books
by Joyce Carol Oates:

Unholy Loves

A Novel by

Joyce Carol Oates

FAWCETT CREST • NEW YORK

UNHOLY LOVES

This book contains the complete text of the original hardcover edition.

Published by Fawcett Crest Books, a unit of CBS Publications, the Consumer Publishing Division of CBS Inc., by arrangement with The Vanguard Press, Inc.

ISBN: 0-449-24457-1

Printed in the United States of America

First Fawcett Crest printing: November 1981

10   9   8   7   6   5   4   3   2   1

for Lois Smedick

Masks are arrested expressions and admirable echoes of feelings once faithful, discreet, and superlative. Living things in contact with the air must acquire a cuticle, and it is not urged against cuticles that they are not hearts. Yet some philosophers seem to be angry with images for not being things, and with words for not being feelings; words and images are like shells—not less integral parts of nature than the substances they cover, but better addressed to the eye and more open to observation. I would not say that substance exists for the sake of appearance or faces for the sake of masks, or the passions for the sake of poetry and virtue. Nothing arises in nature for the sake of anything else. All these phrases and products are equally involved in the round of existence.

—Santayana, *Soliloquies in England*

At the Byrnes'

September 11.

The hour is late, the hour rings with confusion, the voices and laughter of strangers, and something is happening to Albert St. Dennis.

Something is happening to Albert St. Dennis and it is happening, as he has always dreaded, in public; before strangers. At a wild windy improbable edge of the world, quite new to him.

"Something is happening—" an elderly voice murmurs.

Everyone stares. Everyone listens. It seems to him suddenly that an entire continent is his audience. They are greedy strangers, they are memorizing him, storing up anecdotes to be repeated after his death. Tales of the great old poet. Tales of his last days. Final words. Had he wisdom to pass on to the young? Had he visionary calm, authority? The enigmatic utterances of a Blake, the sprawling rhapsodies of a Whitman, the finely toned, bitter, beautiful pronouncements of a Yeats...? But he is only Albert St. Dennis. Only Albert St. Dennis in the frail trembling outraged flesh.

He holds himself stiffly upright as usual. His public posture. His posture before strangers said to be "admirers." He is wearing his good-luck ring—bought at a bazaar in Cairo decades ago, in the company of Maria Huxley—whom he *did* love, as he loved many women, but who did not, contrary to Harriet's accusations, and contrary even to Aldous's sly encouragement, find the time to love him in return: a large old garnet, darkly red, brownish-cherry-bloodstained red, in an ostentatious silver setting, now badly scarified; he is wearing

8

the new green vest (bought at a "men's boutique" on the Kings Road just last week) with the wild aqua designs stitched into it, brave and gaudy, pavonine, like something tossed off by Beardsley in a benevolent mood, mysteriously soiled now but still very attractive, in St. Dennis's opinion. Of course Harriet would not approve; she would say he was descending into "elderly youth" like certain of their friends. (Like Graves, for instance. But then, gossip perhaps exaggerates....) Harriet, however, does not know. There are many things now that Harriet does not know: even St. Dennis's whereabouts must be a mystery to her. (Thirty years ago—or was it forty—St. Dennis spent a surprisingly agreeable evening in the company of Carl Jung, whose theories he had always found rather implausible; but they had talked at length of the dead, of the beloved dead, and Jung had said, it would seem quite seriously, that the dead depend upon the living to give them information—for they know only what they learned while alive, and after their deaths the world continues, knowledge is accumulated, knowledge they require for whatever salvation is to be theirs. But was Jung in earnest? And what sense could one make of all this? Perhaps St. Dennis's skepticism is keeping Harriet from communicating with him.)

In this part of the world strangers listen eagerly to everything he says, and nod with approval. So many faces! So many eyes! Can one be crucified by the simple *attentiveness* of others, St. Dennis wonders. He sputters with laughter. A forthright merry old man, not at all pompous. He wipes spittle from his mouth and realizes suddenly that he will not survive his year in the United States.

Another drink?

The walls of the Byrnes' living room are rosy with smoke and distance. They are fading back into the night, into the wind-tormented foothills of upstate New York. St. Dennis knows where he is: they have told him. They have been very kind, very solicitous. It is all part of the American flummery, perhaps, but helpful nevertheless. Lodgings; apartment-, building-, and office-keys; "group insurance plan"; telephone installed;

a list of services—laundry, shoe repair, pharmacy, The Woodslee Market, even Woodslee Liquor & Wine—and of course a plethora of information about the university, including detailed maps. Back in London, back in the old flat, a slightly trembling forefinger traced his westward route for him, for it would not do to wander about lost, to slip into the vast empty spaces of the New World. Nor would it do, he cautioned himself, to think of the size of the North American continent, for it staggered the mind, taxed the brain, frightened up spirits of confusion and distress. He had known Englishmen decades younger than he who returned from visits to the United States and who spoke of the ineffable terror of the continent: the terror, that is, evoked by one's knowledge of its size, which no map could ever quite adequately suggest. One had to be here, one had to journey to the West Coast, St. Dennis was told. (But he would not journey to the West Coast. Thank you, but no. And some supremely silly woman here tonight has told him he *must* see Hawaii while he is in the States....)

Your first visit here?

And how do you like it?

And how was your flight?

Now that he is over seventy years old he has the right to brush aside such inconsequential gnat-like questions. He knows what he wants to talk about, and he will talk about it. Poetry. The discipline of poetry. The sacrifice. Service. Pilgrimage. He needs only a few intelligent faces about him, he is always stimulated by intelligent faces that are also youthful, and attractive, and the Byrnes have provided him with a small circle of such faces, and he will talk, he will talk. He has sold himself quite shamelessly—and with necessity—to an institution of higher learning some two hundred and fifty miles north of New York City where he will be expected to perform, monkey-like, dancing-bear-like, chattering-parrot-like, and it will give him a kind of perverse pleasure, it is already giving him a kind of perverse pleasure, to speak his mind directly and frankly on all subjects, but particularly on poetry, while people stare curiously at him and listen with concentration, strangers with keen eyes and earnest, innocently cruel faces, storing up anecdotes. Albert St. Dennis. Oh yes. The great poet. The great English poet. Poor man, he seemed somewhat befuddled, he drank too much at the very first party of the year, a party in his honor; yes, to begin with the poor old dear was two hours late and everyone was imagining the worst, yes, and it was *almost* the worst, thank God he hadn't died somehow in his apartment, he had only arrived here, what a scandal it would have been for the university! But he did arrive by cab, already fairly sozzled, and didn't even apologize to his host and hostess but launched immediately on some sort of tirade—about poetry, about Eliot and Auden and Yeats and someone named Bridges and someone named MacNeice—and an old friend of his, Stevie Smith, of whom no one had ever heard—while Marilyn Byrne tried to round us up and herd us into the dining room, futilely, comically—poor gallant Mrs. Byrne, the dean's wife—and there sat as if immobile the great poet himself ("Since Auden's death," says the *TLS,* "the incontestably finest of living English poets") chattering away as if he were at home, and gesturing wildly and nervously, and flicking cigarette ashes (at his age, St. Dennis is a chain smoker) over Marilyn's brushed-velvet love seat, poor dear eccentric withered creature, his eyes a pale washed-out vacuous blue—focused on no one at all. The walls of the living room fell away and we crowded near, a blurred mass of leggy strangers, all of us robust and healthy and marvelously young, taking note of the great man's slurred voice and doughy skin, which soon went dead white from all the alcohol; taking note and applauding everything he said no matter how incoherent it was, no matter how mad or spittle-flecked, for isn't this our role in the comedy?—and isn't that *his* role?

He speaks: Alone among men the poet creates himself. As Yeats knew. Through the strenuous activity of his art. Through the cruel, heart-straining pilgrimage of his art. He risks despair and madness and exclusion from life's feast in order to create his own soul. Alone among men—

11

And now to the dining room? To dinner? It is about to be served—

Another Scotch, St. Dennis says sharply. If you please.

The chunky icy glass soon trembles in his hand. They cannot refuse him, cannot deny him any whim. He has sold himself for a rather stunning sum of money—stunning by his frugal standards, at any rate—and he will play the comedy as he wishes, in the style of, say, Auden or Frost or Oscar Wilde: yes, back to Wilde, why not? In the style of the elderly Isak Dinesen with whom, once, he was unfortunate enough to have dinner, an interminable evening shrill with the vain old woman's monologue. Now it is his turn.

He is arguing with someone. He is defending Yeats, of all people. A long thread of something clings to his fingers as he wipes excitedly at his mouth, and imagines that his new-found admirers are inching in closer in order to stare and memorize. Blind in one eye, growing deaf, embittered by the body's betrayal of the soul— why should Yeats *not* be forgiven anything? Unlike the hypocrite loudmouth Pound, he was an artist. An artist! Incomparable!

St. Dennis interrupts an objection (who *is* that hoarse sweating fool in the corduroy jacket, have they been introduced, will he be a colleague of St. Dennis's, will St. Dennis really be expected to know the names of these people, this horde?) with a brusque motion of his beringed hand, and simply raises his already strident voice, declaiming, in a manner meant to resemble and very gently and skillfully to parody Yeats's own singsong reading voice: *The soul's own youth and not the body's youth/Shows through our lineaments.*

Something about Fascism. The usual. Impertinent spread-bellied opponent, a "professor" of American literature no doubt, challenging St. Dennis in a manner meant, presumably, to be courteous; but really intolerable. The fool! The idiot! Excited, St. Dennis waggles his foot. Old habit. Harriet will scold. Excited, craning his head forward on his skinny neck, dropping ashes. He has drunk too much, he is making a spectacle of himself, he has no shame. Even his accent fascinates these barbaric people, yet he must quarrel—*must* triumph.

So he interrupts and silences his opponent. Crushes him.

Yes, Mr. St. Dennis, the creature says, but—

Crushes him, declaiming fiercely:

> ...Poets, learn your trade,
> Sing whatever is well made,
> Scorn the sort now growing up
> All out of shape from toe to top,
> Their unremembering hearts and heads
> Base-born products of base beds...!

Of course it is an insult—a deliberate insult. But will these people have the wit to grasp it, to interpret it?

Someone over to the left murmurs something about "Irish poetry" but St. Dennis does not hear. He cries triumphantly: "Base-born, base-born, base-born. *Base*-born. Do you see? Eh? Do you follow?"

Base-born, indeed. Base beds. Base. Scorn. His vision narrows swiftly. Someone hands him another drink through a long quavering tunnel. Distant, distant. What time is it, where is he? Far from home? His fingers close greedily about the glass. He remembers: he has bested the squinting staring horde of them with his insight and his passion, he has crushed the paunchy smirking gargoyle-faced opponent, blushing and sullen in defeat but still "smiling" like all Americans ...wanting to be thought good-natured.

Whoever they are, Americans, strangers, hosts, they are slowly flattening out and shifting into two dimensions. Like wallpaper. The colors of their party costumes are oddly faded. St. Dennis's own hands are remote, and his fingernails—what, is that dirt?—dirt black as tar lodged 'neath the nail of his left thumb?—too far away to maneuver. A smudge on his white cuff? Another stain on his handsome vest? His admirers shift uneasily in the glare of his genius, are not accustomed to confronting genius head-on. Diffracted, the light of *their* faces goes flat.

Must speak more calmly. Give others a chance, even the women. Otherwise Harriet will scold.

Must allow a "conversation." "Give-and-take" of ideas. Must appear to listen, even to be impressed....Ah yes. An excellent point.

Is this drink watered? (The stewardess on Pan American played an insidious trick: poured liquor into a glass and then poured it out again and filled the glass with soda and ice. He'd been told they sometimes did this, the clever bitches. He suspected but couldn't prove. Lipsticked smile, typically American, eager to "please." Hypocrite. Their method, an acquaintance said, of controlling undisciplined drinkers. Undisciplined! He, Albert St. Dennis!...And she had been so pretty, so easily effortlessly cruelly pretty.)

Is *this* drink watered as well?

Something is happening. Has been happening. Perhaps he made a blunder, accepting this appointment in North America; perhaps the gods are displeased. He had halfway thought as a younger man that he must never leave England...and Harriet had supported him in this vague superstitious nonsense...palaver about needing his homeland, English soil, Antaeus, that sort of thing. Perhaps there is something to it, he *isn't* altogether himself any longer. The feverish poetic activity a year and a half ago in Rottingdean...the sense of being possessed and used, brutally used, and then abandoned...ah, so *that* is the secret meaning behind Yeats's famous Leda and her swan-lover...! *That* is the secret, perhaps, behind all art: the violent use of the flesh, of any flesh, and then its abandonment. But he had survived Rottingdean. Whatever was happening to him continued to happen, continues even now to happen; life itself is the "untranslatable speech" the poet confronts. (But what will Harriet say about his behavior tonight? He has been rude, insufferably rude. For shame! And he so honored, so admired. Very nearly a sacred relic.)...The frenzy at Rottingdean, the protracted astonishment of his travels, the bomb that fell from the sky that day, that afternoon, in Paddington, decades ago, which he had not deserved to escape but had nevertheless escaped: these mysteries are with him even now, in the New World.

There will be a season of festivities, they have promised him. Parties, celebrations, rituals in honor of poetry. In honor of *him*. (But he dreams nightly of rewriting his poems: book by book by book. Patiently. Cunningly. Rewriting the book of himself and changing not only the private history of Albert St. Dennis but the public events of history as well. He dreams, he cannot help dreaming. Even now, awake, laughing sociably, the dreams of rewriting the world.) He is warmly drunk. He is really quite happy. The mysteries churn inside him, their dreadfulness is familiar, he can live with them as one lives with arthritic joints and a chronically aching knee and eyes that have not been quite right for several years now: he can live with practically anything. Even the persiflage of these silly people.... Should he clear his throat noisily and command them to be still, should he speak to them of the sacred mysteries of his life: not only the agony of creation that August in Rottingdean, when he came so close to death, but the agony of survival during the bombing of London, and the agony of love that has discovered itself sterile (for either he or Harriet was at fault: and too protective of each other and too cowardly to determine the exact nature of the problem), and the earlier vaguer rather comically melancholy agonies of boyhood that seem now to have belonged to another person, a child costumed in the quaint outfits of 1912...?

Certainly not. They would only misunderstand. They would listen eagerly enough but they would misunderstand and in the end they would denounce him. ("Such beautiful poetry—such an ugly man! An imposter! How has he managed to deceive so many of us?")

Is the drink watered? Its effect is paltry. He waits, he waits for something marvelous to happen. Instead the wallpaper trembles, loses its color, goes flat. Seen through the wrong end of a telescope. He takes off his glasses and rubs his eyes. He remembers having been so powerfully impressed by his hosts' house some hours ago that he exclaimed aloud: Is this your private home? This? (Surprise rather than envy; some resentment,

15

perhaps; thinking of the miserable flats he and Harriet rented year after year in London, thinking of the dismal sunless perpetually chilly "maisonette" he now owns in Chelsea.) Such lavish furnishings! That enormous fireplace! Mirrors, a small grand piano, rugs, surfaces that gleam—polished, brilliant, blinding—drapes of pale saffron, silken wallpaper of rich roseate hues. Upon entering the Byrnes' small mansion he felt a thrill of something akin to pure dismay. It was not simply that he was unaccustomed to such elegance, and not even that he rather resented it: he felt instead that he would not be equal to it. As if England itself, the English people as they were now—humiliated, impoverished, frightened of the future—could not possibly be equal to it.

Nevertheless he performed his part, and is performing it still. He is, after all, English. An Englishman. Which means, in the eyes of his gregarious well-intentioned hosts, that he is any number of things they believe they admire, and respect, and even envy. An English poet: the very sound of which calls to mind, to the educated, Milton and Chaucer and Keats and Pope and Shakespeare, of course!—how could one forget Shakespear even for a moment—and Jane Austen and Dickens and—and the man who wrote *Tom Jones*, and the man—woman?—who wrote *The Mill on the Floss*. And of course many others. Many, many others. Kipling, for instance. The British Empire. (On which the sun never set—or so it was boasted.) England and the English and the Tower of London and the Thames and manor houses and castles and ruined cathedrals and churchyards and Stratford-on-Avon and Yorkshire pudding and pence and pounds and shillings and Big Ben and Hyde Park and the Queen and Mr. Pickwick and unheated homes and high tea and Parliament and trade unions and the dole and Piccadilly Circus, which always turns out to be not a circus at all but simply a very busy and very dirty square in the heart of an astonishingly busy and dirty city. Ah, yes. England. Englishman. Poet. Famous? (Someone has told them he is famous—not only in England but throughout the world. And they evidently believed it. And so he must perform his part.)

The ordeal of shaking hands. So very pleased to meet you. And you. Yes. So very pleased. The ordeal of straining to hear: why do these people mumble, is it a sign of awe or of simple bad breeding? The ordeal of smiling. One *must* be courteous, at least at first. Oliver Byrne seems a halfway decent fellow. His wife is quite gracious, despite her almost oppressive desire to please. But there are so many guests. Must he remember them all? Their mumbled names? These strangers who appear before him as if paying homage to an elderly dignitary, declaring their admiration of his work, even insisting upon it (as if sensing his courteous disbelief). Strangers, strangers. And their wives. The dean and his wife. Couples. Affluent and handsome and hopeful. With such remarkably good teeth, on the whole. (*His* teeth—the ones he had suffered with for so many wretched decades—grayish-green, and rotting in his jaws, and the source of such anguish and humiliation!— if these people could have gazed upon his teeth, before they were all wrenched out and replaced with a handsome though extraordinarily awkward set of dentures, how they would pity him, and pass by him in sympathetic silence.)

But of course they don't know, they cannot guess, they are touchingly childlike in their awe of him. And only children, St. Dennis thinks irritably, could be so direct, so crude in their flattery—one of the women told him, her eyes shining, that it was a scandal he hadn't been awarded the Nobel Prize this past year, when everyone—*everyone*—knew he deserved it. Oh yes? Really? How very kind of you to say. And he continued shaking their hands. They were surprised, perhaps, by the strength of the old man's handshake. By his gay good humor. His rather dandyish clothes. He was to be, evidently, a "good sport." Though he had believed he would stay at the Byrnes' only an hour or so, and then beg off, he somehow found himself enjoying the party after all; enjoying the harmless if rather silly adulation; and the dean's excellent Scotch.

After all, these Americans were so eager to honor

him. The educated and articulate and well-to-do members of a nation that barely tolerates the serious arts, and is frankly contemptuous of poetry—how touching that they were eager to isolate and honor *him*. He was a single individual, of course; and it is far easier, and far more pleasurable, to honor a single individual, to award him prizes, prize after prize, than it is to take his discipline seriously in any wider sense, and to be attentive to what others are doing in his field. Yes, he understands; he understands the motive. And in a way he can sympathize with it. For Albert St. Dennis is famous. "Famous" in the narrow hothouse world of letters—whatever letters are—whatever people imagine they are. We can't possess your sensitivity, they murmur, we're practical pragmatic heedless citizens, we skim the surface of life and do it with considerable skill, we don't probe, we don't poke into corners, we never commit suicide, or fall into despair, or into ecstasies— we leave all that to you; and now we're at such a point in history that we won't make you a god and devour your heart, we won't even bother to persecute you; all that has changed, we're quite friendly now, we're no threat.... Mr. St. Dennis, do you hear?

He *wants* not to think such things. He detests skepticism, cynicism. After all, these good generous people have offered him the title of Distinguished Professor of Poetry. And they are demanding very little of his time, it seems: he has been assigned no formal classes, he is expected to give only two public addresses or readings for the entire academic year, and to be on campus only two days of the week. So he *is* grateful. And he *does* like them. But something has been happening as the hours have passed, one drink following another, and these strange uneatable things meant to whet the appetite—mushrooms stuffed with something like liver, tiny fat sausages wrapped in bacon and pierced by festive toothpicks—and the sound of his own excited voice, and the keen frank staring faces that surround him, and the astonishing fact that he is the oldest person in the room, perhaps in Woodslee itself, perhaps in all of New York State; and that he is very far from his Chelsea home.

Dinner? Food?

Isn't it time—?

Another drink?

Mr. St. Dennis was saying—

Quiet, quiet!

What time is it?

He blinks and sees that everyone is still watching him expectantly, like children. Perhaps they *are* children...?

His?

Closest to him, in fact sitting on the floor near his feet, is a most extraordinary young man. St. Dennis cannot quite believe in him: he must be a poet, a flamboyant young rival. His name? His name? Can't recall. Something rather archaic. Hellenic. Heroic. The young man is very young and very blond. Early twenties perhaps. His hair is shaggy, charmingly unkempt, streaked as if bleached unevenly by the sun: predominantly a very light, platinum blond, with streaks of brown. Outrageous. Long straight Roman nose, a firm chin, rather full, sensual lips, striking eyes. The eyes are so brown as to seem red, blood-red, like St. Dennis's garnet. Classic profile. Flawless. Fearless. Beauty. And such chilling confidence—! For the past hour he has been sipping at a drink and staring coolly up into St. Dennis's heated face as if not terribly impressed with the old man's palaver. He sits gracefully, casually, one arm draped about his raised knees, his chin thrust forward. He too is listening, listening closely. But not uncritically. St. Dennis wonders if the young man is being rude, sitting there on the floor like a boy, assuming a kind of intimacy with him that is totally unjustified. And is it appropriate, in any case, that a young person should sit on the floor of the dean's living room, on this special occasion? Or is it a queer American custom? The boy seems too self-possessed to be a student, and yet he is too arrogantly casual, too blatantly glamorous, to be a member of the faculty. He is wearing what appears to be a suede suit, fawn-colored, with a silky green shirt open at the neck; there are several rings on his fingers, and his wrist watch is a solid gold bracelet with a black face and no numerals that St. Dennis can discern. From time to time St. Dennis's foot twitches involuntarily, with the violence of his passionate words, and comes close to touching the young man's knee. But the young man does not draw back, does not flinch; supremely contained, perhaps even a little contemptuous, he sits hugging his knees loosely against his chest, a drink in one hand, eying St. Dennis calmly. Gawky old well-intentioned fool! Let him perform.

A few yards away, facing him, is a young woman who reminds St. Dennis of a beautiful young cousin of his—no longer young, of course, and no longer living. Agnes: two years younger than he. Like this woman, slender, black-haired and black-eyed, too intense, perhaps, too highly wrought. He had always feared that Agnes might kill herself. Might—suddenly—over a weekend, perhaps—kill herself. Of course it was nonsense. Of course he had not mentioned it to anyone, certainly not to Agnes herself. She had died, however, just the same: dead at the age of thirty-two, in a bombing raid in London. The poor girl! She had wanted so much to live, had wanted so passionately to love—and it had not worked out for her, love had failed, loves had failed, she had been bitter and disillusioned while still in her twenties.... Yes, this young woman has Agnes's pale glowing skin, her look of being nervously restrained, almost angry. But Agnes had been rather more beautiful. This woman—her name is Brigit, Brigit something—St. Dennis seemed to recall she was married—and she was an artist, perhaps?—or a writer?—this woman's fine black hair was beginning to go gray in patches, and her thin, faint eyebrows were raised too sharply, as if she were waiting for the right moment to interrupt, to protest. Introduced to her earlier in the evening, St. Dennis had liked her well enough, squeezing her tiny hand in his, noting its damp coldness: ah, she was nervous, as nervous as he! But in fact she does not seem nervous any longer. There is something annoying about her dark, glittering stare. Why are her lips pursed so tightly?—so primly? She too is judging him, she too finds him wanting. Silly old scarecrow, old coat-upon-a-stick! Her occasional smile is perfunctory, her low, throaty laughter is merely conversational. Has she been drinking too much? Where is her husband? He can't recall having been introduced to her husband.

Food?

Ay yes: food.

Mrs. Byrne and a young woman in a white outfit are passing plates around. Be careful, this is quite warm...! The young woman is swarthy-skinned, with thick eyebrows; must be a servant. Somehow St. Dennis did not expect his American hosts to have servants; he did not expect them to acknowledge their servants. Food. Plates. Silverware. Linen napkins. Yes yes yes. Of course. No appetite but one must go through the motions of eating, of pleasing one's hostess. Be careful, Mr. St. Dennis, this plate is quite warm....Can you manage? Let us set this tea table up, it will be more convenient. How's that? Can you manage? Mrs. Byrne with her good-natured smile, her display of gum and strong white teeth, wonderfully American; a woman in an advertisement. He has forgotten her first name. A robust handshake, though, and a good lemony soapy smell. Undisguised pleasure at meeting him. Albert St. Dennis! What an honor! Woodslee's guest for a year, what an honor for Woodslee and for all of us! Ah yes: her name is Marilyn. The dean's wife. Open and sweet and hearty and helpful and motherly, though she is thirty years younger than he, and daughterly too, her eyes filling with tears when they met at the air terminal in Champlain. Tonight he has been a bit naughty, hasn't he, ignoring her timid requests that everyone come into the dining room, refusing to budge, so that no one else budged, and she has been forced to serve her dinner in the living room; naughty old Albert St. Dennis of whom it has been said: *One of the unparalleled poetic geniuses of our time....*

Still, he is naughty. He is capricious. He peers over his eyeglasses at one of his interrogators, as if the man's words were incomprehensible. Yes? Yes? Speak more distinctly!—A question about Eliot. So banal, so predictable. So annoying.

"Tom Eliot...!" St. Dennis says slowly. He means to shake only his head but his entire body shakes, as if in revulsion. "He himself dismissed his work, you

21

know. Swept it aside. As indeed he should have. Adolescent grousing and nothing more and yet you Americans have always taken it so bloody seriously."

The tea table is wobbling. No one speaks, and for the first time St. Dennis notices the watery blood easing from the hefty chunk of beef on his plate. Though no longer a vegetarian, since his doctor told him to forget that foolishness some years ago, St. Dennis eyes the meat with distate. Can it be that these people expect him to eat what they are eating...? Do they expect him to eat at all, while they gape? The brute in the corduroy jacket brings up another subject, he is tireless, now asking about experimental poetry, High Modernism, Eliot and Pound and Yeats and Joyce, wasn't their era long finished, wasn't the word itself more or less finished? Carefully wrought art—wasn't that doomed in the Electronic Age? Aren't we in an entirely new world, nearing the birth of the twenty-first century? Things are happening much too rapidly for them to be assimilated and interpreted, even by artists. And if that is so—

St. Dennis is staring at him. Lewis, the man's name is. He smiles at St. Dennis tauntingly, eating his beef without pause, handling knife and fork with skill. It's remarkable, St. Dennis notes, how the man switches his knife and fork from one hand to the other, not losing a beat in his chewing or in his bullying attention. Close-set gray eyes, a rodent's eyes, fixed steadily on St. Dennis, awaiting his reply. But what can St. Dennis say? Is his craft indeed doomed, is he already extinct, have they brought him to North America as one of the last surviving (and elderly) members of an endangered species...? An aged man is but a paltry thing. And Harriet, could she see, would sharply scold.

Then the dark-haired young woman begins to speak. Her voice is low and cool and throaty, not at all like Agnes's soft girlish voice. She says bluntly: "Mr. St. Dennis, don't feel you must take Lewis's remarks seriously. It's generally known that he says anything that flies into his mind. Sometimes it's brilliant, sometimes it's merely shit. And it's very difficult to distinguish between the two."

Everyone laughs. A few people are startled by the woman's choice of words, and St. Dennis himself is gravely shocked. What on earth did she say! That frail-boned attractive young woman! He finds it hard to believe that he has heard correctly, that she has really spoken such vulgar words in company, unblushing, unhesitant. The comely young blond man grunts his amused approval. Lewis himself flushes a deep angry red but does not reply.

Mrs. Byrne is asking once again if St. Dennis can manage his food.

"Oh my God," he whispers, "leave me alone. I beg you."

"Mr. St. Dennis...?" she says, not hearing.

"Leave me alone," he says, his words slurred, his eyes moist. And then, raising his voice: "You're very kind, Mrs. Byrne. But I can manage very well, thank you. I can manage quite splendidly on my own."

And can she love him, after her days of lurid and humiliating anticipation? She cannot, for St. Dennis is simply too old.

Not merely old but oldmannish. Peering over his spectacles like that...his lips loose and wet and his teeth so obviously and so painfully not his own: ceramic-white, too perfect. No one would ever make teeth like that in North America, Brigit thinks.

She had wanted to love him—to fall in love with him—but it was to be a failure. In spite of the liquor she has had. In spite of her tractable and desperate spiritual condition. Still, his voice *is* beautiful. Papery thin and delicately modulated, the voice of the BBC broadcasts and the single recording she has heard, Albert St. Dennis reading selections from *Hecate* and *Lovesounds*. Perhaps she can half-close her eyes and lose her footing gradually and fall in love with his voice...?

Talk. "Serious conversation." Poetry, the arts, technological America, the future of civilization, the lost *mana* of the poet, the circumscribed condition of the humanities in general, the fact that suicide among young people has increased nearly a thousand percent in the past decade—a fact that St. Dennis appears not to grasp though it is repeated for him. (That none of the rest of us are shocked any longer, Brigit thinks, is a bad sign. But then we've been badgered so much by statistics meant to shock.)...St. Dennis's face is frailboned, tremulous. His skin is soft, softly puckered beneath the eyes, discolored with age and fatigue. The whites of his eyes have gone yellow. The water-color blue of his eyes looks transparent, as if he were really blind; Brigit finds it discomforting to meet his gaze. Suppose he knows, suppose he can guess, her anxiety?—her naive half-angry wish to love him?

Brigit Stott is thirty-eight and Albert St. Dennis is nearly seventy-one, but that should make no difference. Other, odder matches have transpired. She has known of a few; she has heard of many others. He is a widower, and lonely. She is a recent divorcee, and very lonely. And there is something to be said for the eerie depthlessness of those eyes. Imagine sinking into bed with him! Being embraced by him! His hair is thin but unruly, charmingly unruly, and perfectly white. Absolutely white. Colorless. A look of fastidious purity, bone-dry, beyond mortality. (Mortality, Brigit thinks, is the unattractive gray hairs sprouting on her own head. Hairs that are wiry and brittle, unlike the others; unlike what she thinks of as her own hair.)

In her imagination she had already loved him with a sinking-heartedness, a swooning girlish asininity decades outgrown, resurrected now as if to spite her better judgment. But what to make, in the Byrnes' handsome living room, of this skinny old English bird with the potbelly and the trousers with their frayed cuffs and the ragged dirt-edged nails and the clumsy job he did shaving and the querulous drone of his voice and the fact that he is evidently half deaf, or pretending to be so...? What to make of the wattled throat, the trembling hands, the sharp creases in the cheeks, the skull so prominently ridged above the forehead and speckled with liver spots that show evilly through the thin white strands of hair...? The disappointment! The dismay! For she knows, swallowing another large mouthful of her drink, that nothing in her life will be altered. She had hoped for another of her unholy loves—or perhaps it would have turned out holy?—but it will not transpire. Nothing at all will happen.

Brigit Stott had been anticipating this party for weeks. You must come, you are first on our list, Albert St. Dennis will be delighted to meet you, Marilyn Byrne said. Shameful to admit, but Brigit had been thinking of little else. Her course preparations—she would be teaching three courses, one of them an immense section of American literature that would require lectures three times a week—were done hurriedly, early in the day, so she might spend the evening hours thinking and speculating and brooding, sipping a drink, rereading St. Dennis's books. Oliver Byrne had expressed surprise that Brigit owned most of St. Dennis's books, which had irritated her. She told him that St. Dennis's poetry and travel journals and essays and novel (his only novel, dense and all but unreadable, a sort of extended prose poem with a *fin de siècle* weariness, set on a Greek island) were very important to her: genuinely important: she wasn't fabricating enthusiasm like everyone else. She did not tell Oliver how desperately grateful she was to be included in his invitation, nor did she temper her usual coolness toward Marilyn, whom she likes well enough—as she is fond of declaring—but whose inane babble drives her wild.

Surely it must mean something that the Byrnes' party is on September eleventh, a Saturday; and it was on March eleventh, a Saturday, that Brigit was married. Of course that had been some time ago. And the marriage did not turn out as she had anticipated. But Brigit Stott is superstitious, despite her intelligence and her locally famous skepticism; dates are very important to her. As are certain colors (apricot, pale blue, cream), certain odors (lilac, toast, the crass fishy smell of harbors and seashores, new leather, new lumber), music (her mind is clogged with trivial trashy popular songs from her young girlhood, which she sings when safely alone: she *is* ashamed of this weakness), articles of clothing and cities and names and numbers. She is eccentric enough to believe that her superstitions point to a benevolently organized universe; she is willful enough to wish to believe in destiny, but not in fate. When coincidences occur that have an ominous tinge— a lover attired in a fashionable new blazer that is precisely the blazer her husband wore in court, her mother telephoning long-distance to announce, in her plaintive accusatory voice, that an aunt of Brigit's had just "passed away," not an hour after Brigit found herself thinking unkind thoughts about that woman—she brushes it all aside, declaring it folk nonsense, Virginia hillbilly metaphysics.

But she is superstitious, there is no help for it. And despite her hyperborean calm, her somewhat indifferent grooming, her studied look of simply *not caring* about the impression she makes socially, she is really eager, even anxious, to do well socially. She has written novels, she has written innumerable critical essays, she has a small, mild reputation, and is evidently a successful teacher—though she flinches from discussions of teaching and nervously brushes aside all compliments—for if one speaks of something treasured, might it not be lost?—though she is, in others' eyes, an enviable person, it is nevertheless the case that the Woodslee parties are her only solace, her only hope. No one can guess at her loneliness. No, it is more than loneliness: it is a raging ravenous despair, a sort of philosophical despair, as if the drawn-out divorce and the reversal of certain emotions ("love," "tenderness," "compassion") allowed her to see into the depths of the universe itself, and to find it distinctly inhuman. Camus ended his curious little novel *The Stranger* with his psychopath hero's rhapsodic words about the "benign indifference" of the universe, which felt to him brotherly, and comforting; but Brigit, peering into the blank lightless unsubtle abyss outside the human sphere, found nothing benign there, and certainly nothing brotherly or comforting. She wonders: Did Camus himself, dying entangled in a wrecked auto, his blood gushing deliriously free of its confinement, come round to thinking that there might be something malevolent in indifference after all?

Marriage. The deterioration of love. Separation. Reunion. Separation. Divorce. Certain consequences of divorce, unforeseen. No one in Woodslee can guess the degree of Brigit's exhaustion. She has felt, at times, with a remorseless logic, that it might be a good idea for either her or her former husband to die: simply to cease to exist. How cleansing that would be, how generous....As "love" turned inside out to something resembling a furious unremitting "hatred," nearly infantile in its intensity, Brigit like a stunned onlooker at

27

a disaster, wondered at times if she were losing her sanity. It was enough, it was more than enough, that Stanley should turn so passionately vicious: but then she was confronted with her own viciousness, which threatened at times to overleap *his*. And there was the possibility, with which she pricked herself often, that she had made him into what he was now. Certainly he had not been so unjust, so unstable, so mean, in the first stages of their marriage.

A storm of emotions, roused into life and now beyond control. It is true that Stanley seems to hate Brigit more consistently than she hates him, but perhaps that is simply a consequence of her inadequacy as a human being—her infamous anemia, her "frigidity," of which, as their relationship deteriorated, he spoke often in a bitter aggrieved tone, both in private and in public. If he now hates her more wildly than she hates him, perhaps that is to his credit: Stanley would certainly say so. I am a man of deep, intense feelings, he would claim, though he never claimed such nonsense years ago.

But there are parties. There will always be parties. Woodslee is a very social university—detractors might say it is desperately social, because of its isolation, and the long dark merciless winters. Without social life one would simply freeze to death here. Without friends (or the semblance of friends) one would simply die. The Byrnes' party will be followed by another, perhaps at the Seidels'; and then there will be another, and another, and yet another, stretching deep into winter, warming Brigit, keeping Brigit alive. (She will give a party herself this year. Now that the divorce is behind her.) What need to die if there is a party next weekend? So much can happen at a party! Gregariousness dispels all dark somber joyless thoughts. It is, perhaps, our natural condition: and the soliloquies of aloneness, the mere phenomenon of *thinking* itself, are less than natural.

She would like to take St. Dennis aside and speak quite frankly to him. This gibberish about poetry, art, civilization—very impressive, of course—but what about human feeling, what about despair, the utter blankness of the soul? Could he talk her into wanting to live?

Surely—if he tried—this golden-tongued potbellied oracle, gaily drunk, could talk her into anything. If they were alone together she might take his hand, or he might take *her* hand, to comfort her. If he would stop quibbling about old, dead rivals—if he would stop waggling his foot—she might even recite for him a certain poem of Emily Dickinson's, that has been plaguing her for weeks: *This is the Hour of Lead—/Remembered, if outlived,/ As Freezing persons, recollect the Snow—/ First—Chill—then Stupor—then the letting go—*.

(Must decline the next drink. But perhaps no next drink will be offered.)

(Must try not to say offensive things. "Vulgar" things. An innocently contemptuous remark about Anglicanism made last spring at a party given by Lewis and Faye Seidel, uttered within earshot of Vivian Hochberg—whose grandfather is, or was, a bishop in Boston—evidently offended the icy Mrs. Hochberg considerably; and she is, after all, the wife of the chairman of the English department. And once in a crowded place—the foyer of the university theater, in fact—Brigit referred to the president of the university as a *quidnunc*, simply because she liked the word—she liked it, and wanted to use it. But because no one knew its meaning it flew about and could not be recalled, and was, in one of its transformations, the ugly and inexplicable word *queer*—inexplicable in this context, since poor President Garrett has not the imagination for sexual adventures of any kind. Your mouth will get you into trouble one day, missy, people in her family said, and this has already been the case.)

(Must remember to *seem happy*.)

(Must make an effort to be civil to Marilyn Byrne, out of consideration for Oliver.)

(Must draw the conversation, sometime this evening, onto St. Dennis's *The Explorers*, which she wants to ask him about. Not out of flirtatious idleness but out of a genuine curiosity: Has St. Dennis really lived through such experiences? And she should tell him, he will be amused, of her first encounter with *Lovesounds*. Eighteen years old, a freshman at Smith, reading the volume of poetry in the college library, blushing and gasping aloud, shocked into incredulous laughter. She had never come across poetry like this, she had not known that poetry could say such things, do such things. The remorseless cataloguing of the lovers' parts, their mating galumphing parts, as a kind of music-hall song; and the voices of their dismayed spirits as a kind of accompanying dirge. Witty and precise and frank and, yes, vulgar, richly and comically vulgar, even obscene, *Lovesounds* had shocked and offended Brigit at the time (as a girl she was puritanical and is still inclined in that direction), and she remembered thinking how she disliked the poet for his poems and wanted to meet him, to tell him so.)

And now they are together, and he has been looking at her strangely. Dividing his attention between her and Alexis Kessler, sluttish foppish Kessler, the aging *Wunderkind* of the music department, sprawled like an odalisque at the famous man's feet. The conversation is now lively—race relations in America, in England; the situation in South Africa; the scandalous folly of the United Nations—and St. Dennis seems to have given up on his prime rib.

Oddly, Brigit was an hour late to the party. For some reason she had fallen asleep at five, and hadn't awakened until after seven; and then had to shower, shampoo her hair, dress herself, contrive some sort of appearance, snatch desperately for some sort of reasonable face. In a fury of self-loathing, she cursed herself, and chased the cat out of her bedroom and wondered if her stupor-like sleep was a sign of some new illness or a sign, simply, of her spiritual slovenliness. Nothing mattered to her except tonight's party: and so she comes close to missing it. Is it the first step to suicide, after all . . . ? Though she knows herself too cowardly to commit suicide, perhaps the psyche plays tricks, arranges pranks and accidents, and one day death, the unthinkable, comes with the ease of a letter through a slot, or ice cubes bouncing into a plastic container. Suicides are angry people, Stanley once said, reading in the *Times* with grim satisfaction of the suicide—by hanging—of an old classmate-rival. They must be angry to hurt themselves so.

Brigit was an hour late. But St. Dennis was two hours late.

He arrived listing on his feet and mumbling insincere apologies in what sounded like a BBC announcer's voice. Ah, is *that* the great man—! A stubbly chin, unevenly shaved, that reminded Brigit for a moment of her grandfather, long dead; the stale denture odor; watery squinting eyes behind thick lenses; an utterly ludicrous bright-blue vest.

They had all worried about him. As soon as Brigit arrived she realized that no one had missed her, no one had even thought of her, they were all earnestly discussing Albert St. Dennis. Marilyn Byrne wanted to telephone him. But Oliver thought it unwise, for St. Dennis was known to have a capricious temper, and sometimes flew into a rage if he believed his private life was being invaded. Lewis Seidel was arguing in his Bronx voice that it would be no trouble at all for him to drive across town to St. Dennis's apartment; but he would like to call the old man first, and would need his number (which is unlisted, and which the Byrnes have). I could even say, Lewis went on, that we'd arranged ahead of time for him to be picked up. He's probably somewhat absentminded like most poets his age, he wouldn't really remember. But Oliver as the Dean of Humanities was irritated by this suggestion, which smacked of frivolity; though Lewis, pacing about and jiggling his car keys, was hardly joking. (Oliver Byrne and Lewis Seidel had quarreled some years earlier over an "ideological" matter: their rivalry was presented to Brigit as having sprung out of an intense, passionate difference in their philosophies of education. But they rarely quarrel now in public, and the issue remains somewhat mysterious.)

Marilyn Byrne's eyes brimmed with tears. Her house was so lovely, there were flowers, there were hors d'oeuvres about to be slid into the oven, all her guests were here, everyone was drinking, her husband was gravely worried, that awful Lewis Seidel was bullying him and Oliver was too courteous to reply.... Fortunately, Faye Seidel talked her husband out of his plan. Then someone said that Albert St. Dennis might simply have forgotten the date. He might not have marked it on his calendar. Hadn't he a reputation for being somewhat vague about things....But, no, he knew about the party, Gowan Vaughan-Jones stated in his prim brusque voice. He'd run over to St. Dennis's apartment yesterday with a copy of a first edition of *Hecate* for him to sign, and St. Dennis had seemed quite pleased, "almost boyishly pleased," at the prospect of the party in his honor. He had even said something about buying a gift for his hostess, to show his appreciation. What would be appropriate for the charming Mrs. Byrne, he'd asked Gowan.

Then it was said—in fact by Brigit, who dreaded the worst—that something might have happened to him. After all, he was alone in that apartment. He might have slipped in the bathtub, or fallen and struck his head against something hard....Gladys Fetler joined in to say that the poor old gentleman hadn't looked well when she met him the other day. He had been coughing, and spitting into his handkerchief; and for some reason he insisted upon smoking. Lewis Seidel said that he'd heard from friends of friends at Oxford that St. Dennis had had a series of cataract operations not long ago, and was prone to accidents since his wife's death. Which meant that someone should certainly telephone; *he* would be happy to do it.

Warren Hochberg then said in his slow pontifical calm voice that they were being unreasonable. A man of St. Dennis's stature could be as late as he pleased. They could not expect him to contort himself to fit their Woodslee conventions. His wife Vivian added that close friends of theirs at the University of London said that Albert St. Dennis was sometimes late even for poetry readings, and that no one really objected. He was a genius, one must remember.

"Yes, I believe he is a genius," Warren Hochberg said. "I have recently reread all his books and I believe he *is* a genius, somewhere above Auden but below Eliot, and far below Yeats of course." He made this pronouncement in his characteristically ponderous manner, a thumb and forefinger gripping his lower lip, his eyes fixed upon the floor; a picture that stirred Brigit to wonder. As chairman of the English department, Hochberg was an indecipherable personality whom everyone feared, or enjoyed fearing, but Brigit thought perversely that he was rather charming. If one viewed him from a certain angle. She liked it that Hochberg, the author of several well-received scholarly books, and a past president of the Council of Learned Societies, should deliberately impersonate in public a slow-thinking country-headed good-natured oaf.

"Well, we're all geniuses here," Alexis Kessler said. His voice was raw and rude, he meant only to antagonize Hochberg. The Byrnes' guests laughed nervously. One never knew with Alexis whether his acerb comments were genuine, or whether they were a droll form of self-mockery. Brigit stared at him, not liking his outfit. He was resplendent in a taffy-colored suede suit with a green silk shirt open to mid-chest (the sickly pallor of the man's chest was all the more striking in contrast to the frizzy dark curls that sprouted in the V of his shirt); he wore all his usual rings, but had left off, at least, his heavy gold necklace that, rumor had it, was solid gold, a gift from an admirer in Italy; he was drenched in some sort of cologne that smelled like mouthwash; his hair was going dark at the roots because he had neglected to bleach it for some time. Brigit was appalled at the Byrnes' error in judgment in inviting Kessler, of all people, to meet St. Dennis. She would say nothing to Oliver, of course; but she thought it an egregious mistake. She was herself a writer—a failed writer, in her own estimation—but a writer nevertheless, with a small reputation—while Alexis Kessler was a former musical prodigy, long burned-out, long exposed, now a spoiled child whose disdain for his colleagues at Woodslee was notorious, and whose jealousy of their successes was legendary. Seeing him there in the Byrnes' living room, Brigit had felt her heart sink. Oh that bastard, she had thought. She detested men with pretty faces.

And then she was somewhat disoriented by having slept so long, and by the manic haste of the past hour. How odd, how very odd, that she should have fallen asleep, and should have found it so difficult to wake

33

up.... These bouts of sleep were becoming disturbingly frequent. She might teach a most agreeable class, manage to intercalate all the small clever "casual" details she'd hoped to during the course of the fifty minutes; she might feel gloriously alive, alert, invincible; and then, back in her office or back home, the drowsiness would sweep upon her.... At first it was warm and comfortable, like inhaling the smell of fresh-baked bread (another of her cherished odors); but then, quickly, it became overwhelming. She was suddenly exhausted, deathly exhausted, and must lie down at once, without even taking the time to undress. And in sleep she was pitched down, down, far down. She did not dream, or did not remember dreaming. Sleep struck like a blow, a sword. It was utterly blank and featureless, though when she tried to describe it she spoke of it as muddy. The muddy floor of an unfathomable ocean, where nameless faceless bodies are rolled gently over and over, helpless and mute and perfectly at peace. But it was not really the sleep that terrified her, but the difficulty with which she woke. She had always been an insomniac—she had rather prided herself on her insomnia, imagining it betokened a pristine sensitivity.

Perhaps St. Dennis could give them a little lecture on sleep? There was a poem of his.... What was its title.... A chilling sonnet that drew together Plato, and the gardens of Adonis, and the dead of World War II. Brigit had been reading about sleep and death and the soul and consciousness a great deal recently, and hurriedly too, as if time were running out for her. She had become fascinated by the phenomenon of consciousness itself. She read books by neurophysiologists, she reread *De Anima*, and even Schopenhauer, and Erich Neumann, who described in such detail the labor of consciousness, of becoming human: the gravitational pull each individual feels toward sleep, the unconscious, the original Uroboros: the cessation of all conflict. In the end, though, more than the others Neumann succeeded only in making her pathologically drowsy.

And so it was 8:30 and then 8:45 and then 9:00 and then 9:20 and Brigit consoled Marilyn Byrne, hearing herself say banal reassuring false things, feeling herself stretch her lips into a smile. The mask, the cuticle, the necessary gesture. She isn't quite willing to admit that she envies Mrs. Byrne—envies the woman her attractive husband, and her settled position in life—how relaxing it would be not to be fired by a compulsion to "create"—simply to live, to consume, to decorate rooms and plan dinner parties and blink tears out of one's eyes when the guest of honor fails to appear!—but she is willing to admit that Marilyn had been extremely helpful and generous to her. During the worst months of Brigit's disastrous marriage she had telephoned several times a week, she invited Brigit to the City Women's Club for lunch, asked her for sisterly advice about clothes and furnishings and other claptrap, and which people might be invited along with which people to parties (for, as the dean's wife, she was constantly entertaining; and as the dean's wife she was somewhat sheltered from, or deprived of, the delightful claver everyone else trafficked in); she invited Brigit to join her at meetings of Amnesty International, Planned Parenthood, the Woodslee-Champlain Environmental Commission. Brigit declined these invitations but was grateful for them. Had Marilyn Byrne saved Brigit's life? It would not do to think so.

Waiting for Albert St. Dennis. Who must have left his apartment, who must be en route to the Byrnes', for Oliver finally weakened and telephoned; but there was no answer. Waiting for the great man, and drinking too much, and breaking into peals of unaccountable laughter. Twenty-five people. Most of them were familiar to Brigit, a few of them—Lewis Seidel, for instance—rather too familiar, since their offices in the Humanities Building were adjacent, and they were invited to the same parties. But two couples were new. They were also young, dismayingly young. Brigit was introduced to them but mixed up their names immediately, and for the rest of the evening could not remember who was who, or who was married to whom. Barry and Ernest. Carol and Sandra. The Jaegers, the Swansons. The men were both assistant professors in the department, new appointments whose vitae she had evidently studied, though she could remember nothing.

Barry Swanson, Ernest Jaeger. Or was it Barry Jaeger and Ernest Swanson? Both wore glasses. Both were quite nicely dressed—the taller of the two in a herringbone suit with a vest, the kind of outfit Brigit's husband liked to wear when things were really bad with him; he believed, as Brigit had come to believe, that the more wretched one felt, the more conspicuously elegant one dressed. What was distressing was the youth, the actual boyishness, of the two young professors....One of the wives, Carol, was vivacious and rather intimidating in her snug white dress; a moderately pretty girl with a jarringly loud laugh, evidently of Italian or Greek descent; Brigit might envy her spirit, her zestfulness. But the other wife, Sandra, was strikingly beautiful. Really, there was no one like her at the party tonight, on one like her in Woodslee. Fine cool unperturbed features, silky blond hair expertly cut to swing loose at the level of her chin, large gray eyes, lovely mouth. She was beautiful and knew it, and Brigit could not help glancing at her, like certain others—Lewis, for instance—and even Alexis Kessler, who might have sensed a rival. Ah, to be that age again, with a kind tender intelligent promising young husband!—to be that age again and to look like *that*. Brigit could not help herself, she did envy the young woman. In fact she envied all four young people.

A world of married lovers.

Might she have another drink...?

No one watching. Bar set up at the far end of the living room, French doors opened onto the flagstone terrace, a pleasantly cool September night. There was Oliver Byrne laughing uneasily at an anecdote spun out by Lewis Seidel (an anecdote not about St. Dennis but about another year's distinguished professor, the sculptor Myron Tyne, who had presented some grave problems to the administration, and who even—so gossip had it—was roughed up by the Woodslee city police); there was another colleague of Brigit's, Gladys Fetler, deep in conversation with someone's wife. Miss Fetler was one of the senior members of the department, a popular teacher, a Shakespeare scholar, of whom it was said—invariably—that she made Shakespeare "come alive"; she was sixty-three years old and gracious and ladylike and kindly and youthful, and from the start she'd been extremely friendly to Brigit—who had drawn back from her, not wanting intimacy, not wanting maternal compassion. When they meet, Gladys is always hearty and Brigit is always shy, and nervously guilty. She *should* allow Miss Fetler to befriend her.... But somehow she always eases adroitly away, and feels ashamed of herself afterward.... What a marvelous person Gladys Fetler is, everyone says. Students love her, she's still publishing (her most recent publication is a note on the staging of Webster's *White Devil*, in PMLA), she has these wild wacky hobbies—mountain-climbing, bird-watching treks into the Everglades and into the Arctic Circle, canoeing in the White Mountains. And she's reticent about her religion, which is also something odd: Seventh-Day Adventist or Christian Science: she's such an obviously *good* person.

I can't bear good people, Brigit said. Afterward she wondered if her remark made its way back to Miss Fetler.

Brigit found herself in a conversation with Oliver Byrne but it was disappointing—about the university senate, quarrels over budgets, parking-lot assignments, library privileges. Then he asked if she were going home to Norfolk for Christmas. (So soon? Questions about Christmas so soon?) The youngish Dean of Humanities possessed a golden smile, a toothed charming glow; his suits were impeccably tailored; if he turned discreetly aside to wipe his nose, it was a white linen handkerchief with which he wiped it—no lurid pink or yellow Kleenex for Oliver Byrne. He has the air, a jealous detractor once said, of yet another Kennedy sibling. Brigit told Oliver curtly that she certainly was not. Five days last December were quite enough, as she might have mentioned to him—for she and Oliver were friends, of a sort—it flattered her that he appeared to be mildly and half-mindedly attracted to her, and she tried to make herself feel something, feel anything, in the presence of a handsome man, if only to assure herself—contrary to her husband's accusations—that she was a normal woman. But though

Oliver initated "personal" conversations with his faculty, behind his encouraging smile and the intelligent blandness of his blue gaze he often mixed people up; and Brigit saw that he simply could not remember the evening he and Marilyn had consoled her. But then, perhaps, they consoled so many Woodslee misfits.

Someone else joined them, ice cubes clinking in his glass, and the subject was the discouraging fall enrollment: perhaps if publicity had gone out earlier on the new fine arts program, and the work semester in South America, and the poet-in-residence St. Dennis—?

Brigit pretended to listen. She could pretend as well as anyone, she was quite skillful at parties, and knew that all one had to do was stand near people who were talking animatedly; one could then daydream or brood as one wished.... How annoying, that Oliver had asked her about Norfolk. Brigit's mother, Brigit's father, Brigit's younger sister Janet (who has been married now for fifteen years, a mother twice over, and altogether content—*Look at Janet*, Brigit's mother whines, *she made a success of her marriage without even trying*), too many Stotts who had nothing to do but drop by the house and inquire after Stanley. Stanley who had always "seemed so courteous." "Seemed so gentlemanly." Brigit's was the first divorce in the family since someone's great-uncle back in 1923 sued his runaway wife for desertion—she had fled to Texas, family legend had it, in the company of a dusky-skinned, suspiciously thick-lipped itinerant photographer; in El Paso, the tale went, she had died of food poisoning before the divorce had even been settled. So the Norfolk Stotts eyed Brigit, seeing not the thirty-eight-year-old university professor and novelist, seeing, in fact, not a thirty-eight-year-old woman at all, but just Brigit, Hannalee's oldest daughter, the "strange" one, the "bookish" one (Janet was the "popular" and "pretty" one, of course) who had insisted upon going North to school and who had rashly married a New Yorker after only a few months' acquaintance and who had written two or three peculiar books—what kind of books would you call them?—fiction?—or was it poetry?—and who had separated from her husband and was divorcing him, for reasons not made clear—but then Brigit was always headstrong and mouthy and wouldn't have the first idea of how to make a man happy.

A world, Brigit notes bitterly, of marriages. Yes, everyone has declared himself—or herself—liberated: and so they were "liberated" for a few years. In the mid-seventies. It felt good for a while, it felt exquisite, why hadn't anyone known about this before? But then, after some years, it no longer felt quite so good; couples were discreetly forming once again, newer couples, new combinations, surprises. One by one people were hooking up with mates again. Taking refuge in each other. The most astonishing combinations, in fact.... Brigit, however, does not want to marry again. She loathes the very idea of it. And her divorce is not *quite* final yet—there is still the vestige of a union—as if part of her soul were in bondage to a stranger. As if someone, his name unknown, his face unknown, someone in this very room perhaps, were staring at her secretly, staring right into her head and discerning her thoughts. (As Stanley once boasted of doing. I can read the thoughts rising like bubbles in your brain, he said, plagiarizing Pope; which had exasperated Brigit all the more.) She does not want to marry again, not in any conventional way.... Yes, but: but perhaps in another way?

So her mind turned and turned upon Albert St. Dennis, stimulated by the several photographs of him she owned, on book jackets: not a handsome man but attractive, very attractive indeed. Deep-set eyes, a thin-lipped calm smile, not a smile so much as an indentation, a gesture. Of course the photographs were dated now, the most recent one had been taken in 1952, but perhaps.... And then Brigit has never been the sort of woman to admire physical appearances....

She does not want to marry again, she has said so, frequently and passionately; and yet some sort of alliance with a man like Albert St. Dennis....

He would be one of her holy loves. She has had holy loves, and unholy loves. Very few of the former; too many of the latter. And then, quite inexplicably, certain of the former—notably her husband—evolved into

39

the latter. But Albert St. Dennis is in a sense immortal and she can see herself as his bride. Made young again, or young-seeming. Albert St. Dennis and the American novelist Brigit Stott. Why should it *not* happen, when preposterous things happen so routinely these days...?

It is because of such adolescent fantasies that Brigit has come to dislike herself sharply these past few months. She knows better, certainly; she *knows* a great deal; and yet her imagination swerves to such idle hopes, such pathetic aspirations. Of course she isn't drifting into madness. Madness has always struck her as slovenly and exhibitionistic, and a great deal of trouble for other people. If one had concern for others one would *not* go mad; it seems to Brigit as simple as that: a moral choice. Instead she fears that she is becoming weak and callow and sentimental. Stanley had knocked certain daydreams out of her, and she knows herself well rid of them. Yet now new dreams threaten. It would be quite in order for Brigit Stott to fantasize about her career—completing a lengthy essay on Henry James she had begun eighteen months ago, completing her novel and delivering it to her publishers by next May (she promised this novel to them in May of four— or is it five—years back); she might even fantasize shamelessly about its being well-recieved in the press and read by numerous sympathetic people, a few of whom would take the time to write her—the only really pleasing consequence of her first two novels, published long ago. (By now, Brigit supposes, the people who had liked those novels are dead, or inoperative.) She does not dare to fantasize about the novel's being widely acclaimed, since the acclaim attending the first (an austere girlhood novel, obliquely autobiographical), and to a lesser extent the second (an analytical first-person narrative set inside a doomed marriage), back-fired on her in certain dismal ways, some of which she has yet to comprehend. She might, however, fantasize that the completion of the novel—she has come to think of it as wretched—that wretched novel—might bring to an end this unhappy phase of her own life. All these fantasies, while silly, would be at least respectable.

Instead, her imagination turned about the figure of

Albert St. Dennis. And as she drank, awaiting the famous man, no longer listening to the edgy conversations surrounding her, no longer bothering to seem interested, her imagination took on feverish energies: here, in this very room, before a small crowd of university people, she, Brigit Stott, was to be introduced at last to Albert St. Dennis. The way they grasped each other's hand, the way they smiled—startled, pleased—as if recognizing each other—though of course they had never met before—would be keenly noted by all. The Byrnes and the Hochbergs and the Seidels and the Haases and the Tomlinsons and the Housleys and Gladys Fetler and Gowan Vaughan-Jones and the Ryersons and the Swansons and the Jaegers and whoever else was present—ah, yes, Alexis Kessler—would all be witnesses. St. Dennis would be very like his photographs: a beautiful old man, white-haired, with fine, noble cheekbones, a warm and gracious manner, surprisingly quick to laugh, however, and witty, and energetic, and obviously in superb physical condition for a man of his age—rather like Picasso, people would say afterward; or Pablo Casals; youthful but certainly dignified, with a steady, sometimes stern gaze—he had no patience with fools, not this old gentleman. Beautifully dressed, again as his photographs suggested: watch chain, vest, full resplendent necktie, interesting ring—was it an antique, had it any sentimental or superstitious meaning? (Brigit would find out.) A remarkable man. A genius. A kind of saint, in fact. His innumerable honors and awards meant nothing to him, it seemed; he dismissed them with an embarrassed wave of his hand; he was (so he would confide in Brigit) at work on the only significant poem of his life—a sequence even greater than *The Explorers*—a work that would rank higher than *The Wasteland* in the estimation of future lovers of poetry. (But would so modest and self-aware a man as St. Dennis actually say such things to Brigit...? Perhaps not.) A kind of saint, in any case. Generous with his time, his money, his attention. But lonely, since his wife's death. (When had the wife died? Brigit seemed to think it was only a year or so ago: she had come across a tiny obituary

41

somewhere, *Harriet Arnold St. Dennis, 65, after long illness, London, England. Married to the poet Albert St. Dennis. A poet herself, having published several books in the thirties....*) Yes, lonely since his wife's death. Very lonely.

Introduced to Brigit Stott, he would be struck by her face, by something in her face. Her fine dark eyes, perhaps. Her enigmatic expression. He would be bringing with him warm greetings from the president of the English publishing house that brought out both their books in England, and possibly from Brigit's editor as well. (Though she was not certain that the young man who had worked with her novels, years ago, was still with that house. Everyone moved around so much in English publishing circles; and she had heard a rumor, a while back, about his having been fired.)...St. Dennis would have been anticipating their meeting, perhaps, as she had anticipated it. Perhaps a friend had given him one of Brigit's novels to read, perhaps it had been his wife, even, who had discovered this quiet, slender, impeccable talent, and who had pressed upon him *Worlds Elsewhere* or *Melodies*, insisting he must read it: it was so exquisitely beautiful, so classically restrained and yet so moving. Very likely it was *Melodies* he had read, since that had sold a little better than *Worlds Elsewhere*, which had been misconstrued as a sort of low mimetic science-fiction work, though it was, in fact, about genteel life in Virginia. Yes, it would be *Melodies*. He would have been struck by the dust-jacket photograph, perhaps, Brigit in her late twenties, wan but quite lovely, undeniably lovely....And of course the Byrnes would have told St. Dennis about her. One of Woodslee's outstanding talents.

"I'm very honored to meet you, Miss Stott," he would say softly. "Very honored...."

Everyone would be watching, everyone would be listening.

A historic meeting, in a sense.

Albert St. Dennis and Brigit Stott.

Seated beside her at dinner he would pay attention to no one else. Utterly fascinated, charmed, as only a distinguished man might be, willing to make his interest in a woman quite public, since he is so confident of himself. Unashamed of emotion. Lesser men would deny their interest in a woman if it swept upon them so violently, since they would be alarmed by it; but St. Dennis, the author of *Lovesounds* and *Hecate* and *The Brides of Rain* and *The Explorers*, was equal to his own passions. Like the heroes of his long poem, he was an explorer of his own fate, his own destiny, and did not draw back from a love affair with a woman so very much younger than he....

He falls in love. Tonight.

In the days that follow he pursues her, with the self-conscious, mildly ironic gallantry of old age. *Why should not old men be mad?* He will quote Yeats. He will quote Yeats desperately, laughingly: *Because I am mad about women/ I am mad about the hills....A young man in the dark am I,/ But a wild old man in the light....I forget it all awhile/ Upon a woman's breast....* But no: why would he quote Yeats to her? He would compose his own poems. A sequence of poems, perhaps. For her. For Brigit. For my love, Brigit. For my darling Brigit. For my wife.

But now events accelerate: he pursues her, writes the poems, marries her, they return to England. They are a devoted couple. Everyone is amazed. Brigit Stott puts aside her own work and dedicates herself to Albert St. Dennis. She wishes to make his old age as comfortable as possible. She helps him with his manuscripts, types for him, does proofreading for him, reads galleys, meets with agents and editors and interviewers and professors, protecting him, her own work quite forgotten. An exceptional marriage. Noted by all. The envy of everyone. She entertains in their charming Chelsea maisonette; she is a tireless hostess, bringing a certain American vivaciousness, a certain Southern flirtatiousness and combativeness, to these famed social evenings. All of literary London attends. New Yorkers fly over, simply to visit. St. Dennis's new poem is finished, parts of it have been appearing in the *TLS* and elsewhere, and it is immediately acclaimed as his major achievement, and one of the great achievements of the twentieth century. He is praised everywhere.

Translated into many languages. He gives readings, lectures, addresses. Accepts more prizes. Accepts a knightship (if that is the word—Brigit groggily isn't sure). Of course his young wife accompanies him everywhere. It is rumored that she helped him compose his brief but memorable Nobel Prize address. How astonishing that she should abandon her promising career for him, that she should so efface herself in the service of his art.... And there is no question but that the two are genuinely in love. "Behind Albert St. Dennis stands Brigit Stott," people will say. "She saved his life, you know. A remarkable woman...."

"Sometimes it's brilliant," Brigit hears her drunken voice declare many hours later, "sometimes it's merely shit...."

Too late she sees the old man's displeasure; but she cannot stop; despite the subtle change in the atmosphere about her (others are displeased, not just St. Dennis) she must follow through with her point.

Lewis hardly minds. In fact it delights him to be publicly attacked. Now he has an excuse to launch into a fifteen-minute lecture, a noisy swaggering harangue, sweeping all "consciously wrought," "aristocratic" art into the abyss, naming names with the zest of a triumphant guerrilla leader: Proust and Valéry and Nabokov and Mann, and of course Virginia Woolf, Henry James, Joseph Conrad, Yeats and Eliot and Pound and Auden and Lowell and Stevens and Faulkner and Hemingway and—Modernism is dead, faith in literature itself is dead, absolutely dead, even *Finnegans Wake* came too late, for hadn't Joyce realized—as Lewis had himself realized, irrevocably—that literature ended with the publication of *Ulysses*, with the publication of—nay, the very conception of—such episodes as "Wandering Rocks" and "Cyclops"—? No, no, it does no good to argue, no good at all! Literature is dead. Exhausted. We have now a kind of meta-literature, shoulder shrugs and vaudeville routines and grimaces, schoolboy stuff, but honest just the same, willing to acknowledge its fatuity, its futility. He, Lewis Seidel, had been a Modernist without knowing it, an elitist, grimly faithful to

44

the Word, to the intellect, refusing to acknowledge the fact—which the young had acknowledged so blatantly in the sixties—that the Word has been replaced by the Sound or the Image, the soundless Image or the imageless Sound, sheer sensation, and the intellect has been replaced by the instincts, and in the future there would be no "art" at all in the sense in which we know it, only random improvised experiences, bits and particles of sensation, brute sensation—

Lewis speaks passionately. St. Dennis, gray-faced, one eyelid drooping lower than the other, appears to be listening; he sits with his liver-spotted hands meekly in his lap. Most of the others, who have heard Lewis's ideas before, are waiting patiently for him to finish. He usually finishes by quoting Wittgenstein, though sometimes he quotes Heidegger, in German. Faye Seidel, plumper than Brigit remembers, and looking as distressed and apologetic as usual, is going to try to calm down her husband; Brigit can see the poor woman's hand twitching—she wants to touch his arm, wants to reach over and touch his arm, lightly, but does not dare—it was said that he had once struck her for trying to quiet him, in a similar situation, at a party in Myron Tyne's studio. Marilyn Byrne, hovering hostess-like behind St. Dennis's chair, is waiting for the proper— the exact—moment: when Lewis pauses to catch his breath she will lean down to whisper in St. Dennis's ear, to ask him—not whether he'd like more wine, surely?—not more food, he has simply messed about on his plate Marilyn's superb dinner—perhaps if he'd like to stretch his legs, walk out onto the terrace with her—? And there is the prospect of some music, to change the situation entirely. (Brigit was told earlier that Alexis might be persuaded to play one of his compositions for them. Though Brigit is not looking forward to hearing a Kessler extravaganza, she hopes for Marilyn's sake that he will play and save the evening.)

Poor Albert St. Dennis! Trapped there behind the wobbly tea stand, a quite ordinary-appearing old man, shabbily English, his hair poorly cut and his oversized spectacles slipping down his nose. He has not been following Lewis's argument, just as the others have

45

stopped following it, but for reasons of his own: he appears to be nonplused, annihilated. Brigit hopes he hasn't *believed* Lewis's remarks.... He is a terrible disappointment to her, of course, hardly the lover-savior she had anticipated, just an old man, a sick-looking old man. Genius, no doubt—or had been once. And possibly nicer, kinder, than he has appeared tonight. (So blustery and bullying and oldmannish earlier, shouting people down, defending Yeats needlessly, chanting *base-born* at his hosts and new colleagues as if he were chanting a curse against all Americans.) He is not the lover Brigit's feverish imagination contrived, but he is likable, she likes him, she hopes they will be friends. And now he really must be rescued from Lewis....

But Marilyn misses her opportunity, her own husband interjects a comment, as if he were taking Lewis seriously, and so the discussion continues. Gowan Vaughan-Jones is drawn in and is easily rebutted by a prankish Seidel; Alexis Kessler mutters something that sound vaguely concurring; the beautiful young woman, Sandra, whose last name Brigit has forgotten, stares at Lewis open-eyed, her slender fingers actually closed upon—ah, how Brigit is pierced by envy!—her husband's wrist, as if she felt him threatened, yet could not resist his opponent's massive satyrish charm.

Brigit finds herself studying Alexis Kessler. She must ask Oliver why on earth he was invited; hadn't there been rumors last year that the dean was maneuvering to ease him out on account of some small scandal or other: students and drugs and missed classes and outrageous impertinence (Kessler was the one who turned in to the University Committee on Promotion, Tenure, and Status a blank sheet of paper on which he had scrawled an obscene imperative in red ink, instead of a dutiful listing of his activities and publications during the preceding academic year). There are rumors about everyone at Woodslee, of course; Brigit even suspects there may be a few about her, but since she leads so conventional a life the rumors must be dull indeed; but the rumors about Alexis are particularly savage. And he does nothing to refute them. Look at those epicene features, that outrageous bleached hair, not even *well*-bleached. Look at the tight trousers, the exposed chest hair, the innumerable gold-glinting rings. His idle contemptuous expression....Brigit, sipping her drink, stares at him. If he notices she does not care: she too can be rude. He *is* a very handsome man. A boy-man. In his late twenties. A *Wunderkind*, a prodigy. One of those very young debuts (as a pianist), and afterward it must have gone to his head, all the attention, the admiration and applause and fuss.... His first compositions were performed in public, and even recorded, before he was in his twenties. Quite by accident Brigit had seen a ballet of his in a Village theater once—talked into going by friends of hers and Stanley's, though both she and Stanley disliked avant-garde art—and she had been impressed, not altogether negatively, by the outrageous demands Kessler's music had made upon the dancers. (The ballet had been a grotesque satire of some sort about contemporary American life: Brigit remembers immense ugly papier-mâché masks, and plaster heads and shoulders, and people tottering on built-up shoes like drunken giants, a great deal of percussive sounds, whistles and drums and horn and hissing noises and sudden startling blackouts. The ballet had been fairly controversial. At least the *New York Times* Arts and Leisure section had treated it as controversial. Brigit could not recall whether the production was successful or whether it failed miserably and closed after a few weeks.)

So he is prodigious, and talked-about. Brigit has heard people refer to him as a genius. That he is talented she has no doubt, that he is a genius she refuses to acknowledge; no one younger than she could possibly be a genius....And he is in retreat up here at Woodslee, which suggests that things haven't gone well with his career. Like Brigit herself he is, perhaps, in hiding. (But Brigit, unlike Alexis, leads a quiet life, a near-monastic life.)

The rest of the party dims; the others become two-dimensional. Even Lewis's voice fades. Alexis Kessler with his shaggy blond mane, his lean body, his slender arms and wrists...his somewhat sullen expression... the affectation of his watch, which glows a sinister purple-black and seems to have no numerals or hands.... Tight-fitting suede trousers, stylish custom-made shoes, bared chest, rings (one of them is topaz, Brigit notes suddenly: rather like a ring of her own, a precious, sentimental piece of jewelry bound up with her girlhood and a friendship that had meant a great deal to her) on several fingers, fingernails fastidiously manicured. He is dandyish, sinister, silly, frightening. Not male and not female. A purely sensual being: frightening. His body seems to exclude personality. His body *is* his personality. She is attracted to him in a way. From time to time he glances at her, as if sensing her interest. In a moment Marilyn will lean down to St. Dennis and the scene will be altered, they will be freed of Lewis's overheated intensity, everything will be changed. Brigit stares quite frankly at Alexis now. She is not really attracted to him—she feels, instead, a fascination for him, a curious impersonal revulsion. He is so glamorous and yet so sleazy. He is so handsome a young man, and yet so unmanly. Affecting a kind of childlike innocence, and yet the rumors that fly about his head—! Someone in New York, a dancer with the Martha Graham Company, had evidently committed suicide over Alexis a few years back; or was it a prominent director in the theater...? A man, of course. And Alexis had fled, had had a breakdown of some kind, had disappeared and then reappeared, not very changed, a little quieter, perhaps, a little less brazen. He had come to Woodslee a year before Brigit. Again and again they have met each other, at innumerable parties they have been thrown together, have even been seated beside each other at dinner. Two artists, after all. A failed novelist and a musician-composer who is—perhaps—not quite a failure, not yet, but not a success either. Staring at him, Brigit tries to recall why she dislikes him in a specific, personal way; had he insulted her once...? She dislikes him as a being, as a creature, as an appearance: his deliberately sensual manner, his presentation of himself as an arrogant, self-important artist, a pretty face, accustomed to arousing emotion in others without being required to express any himself.... She sees in him an earlier form of herself, the petite and almost pretty Brigit Stott of Norfolk, a high-school girl, rabidly self-conscious, vain, desperate to be admired. She sees in him something that defies her, as not even Lewis Seidel defies her, or her own husband with his wild charges of infidelity and his promises to make her "regret" everything defies her—and she feels inexplicably moved, stung, annoyed. He glances at her unseeingly. He is being *seen*; he has no need to see anyone else. There is no one at the Byrnes' tonight worth Alexis Kessler's attention except, in a way, Albert St. Dennis, at whom he has been gazing for a very long time.

Brigit recalls having studied Alexis in the past, at one or two other parties. Always she was repulsed, disturbed. She has no interest in younger men, for one thing, and has always been mildly baffled at the fact that any woman could be attracted to any man younger than she—wouldn't it be a kind of incest, like brother and sister? And then, he is not really a man; not really. There have been occasional rumors about his involvement with women, even with girl students at the university; but Brigit is inclined to discount them. She doubts that a normal woman would be attracted to Alexis Kessler.

As for his music....

She really should not judge because she knows herself unmusical. She can barely grasp the musical logic of Bartok, and is quite at a loss to comprehend such radical and odd-sounding developments as twelve-tone compositions, and electronic symphonies, and the discomforting silences of John Cage and his protegés. She should not judge and yet she cannot resist: Kessler's music *sounds* unmusical to her ears. Like objects falling off a shelf, she once said wittily, glasses and plates and pots and pans....It crossed her mind that the remark must have been repeated to Kessler, but she did not regret having made it.

Most of the time, when they meet, Alexis greets her vaguely and then ignores her, but tonight Brigit is struck by the hostility in his face. There is a sharp unattractive line between his eyes—he had better be careful, she thinks, he will lose his looks. Their uneas-

iness with each other began some time ago. As a new
member of the English department Brigit was introduced to the rest of the faculty at the president's reception, always held near the start of the academic
year, and by accident she drifted into a group that included Alexis Kessler. She had not known who he
was—she hadn't remembered the name—but the occasion was exhilarating, she had had several glasses
of excellent champagne and was feeling quite hopeful
about her new life; and so she had found herself talking
animatedly with Kessler. She had *felt* like an attractive
woman that night. (She and Stanley were living apart
at the time, but he had not yet become hateful.) And
of course Alexis was capable of being extraordinarily
charming when he wished.

They went to a buffet table together. He handed her
a plate. She happened to notice his hands—how filthy
they were—actual webs of dirt between his fingers. The
nails were clean enough, even polished, and his outfit
was fashionable and probably quite expensive. But his
hands were filthy. Brigit, unthinking, had exclaimed,
"Oh, look at your hands—do you know your hands are
dirty?" and Alexis, unhesitating, had smiled coldly at
her and said, "If you think my hands are dirty, lady,
you should see the rest of me." He had spoken in an
utterly calm, jeering voice.

The bastard.

Remembering, now, she shivers with dislike of him.

Brigit touches Lewis's arm. "Enough, enough," she
says, her voice hoarser than usual, "too much," and she
gets to her feet and stretches, rather rudely, not caring
what anyone thinks. This party is not going to change
her life after all: what does she care any longer what
anyone thinks?—even the guest of honor?

Once he was beautiful; now he is merely pretty.

Once a probable genius—now, merely talented.

Still, he is playing this difficult piece for the Byrnes' guests as if his reputation depended upon it, as if his very life—his life as an artist—depended upon it. He is playing and they are listening. Music: the rapid, percussive notes: the sudden deep chords: a kind of triumph that might redeem him.

And Albert St. Dennis is here tonight.

Alexis plays, hunched over the keyboard of the Byrnes' baby grand, beginning to perspire. The room is too warm, and his outfit is too warm. He has been nervous for hours. Not simply the prospect of meeting St. Dennis, after all these months, but the prospect of the party itself had unnerved him: he dreads these Woodslee evenings, these hearty gatherings in one or another couple's home, hour after hour of amiable trivial chatter in which he can't successfully participate. He is well aware of the veiled stares of his colleagues and of their courteous dislike of him. Several of these people frankly hate him—he knows that; he would swear to it. There was a move of some kind to fire him not long ago and only the dean's humane intervention saved him. Alexis isn't sure, but he believes it was the president of the university himself, Garrett, who wanted him fired.... Why? He didn't know. Doesn't know even now. Matt Ryerson, the head of the music department and a supposed friend of his, has never explained the ugly situation satisfactorily to Alexis. He suspects that Garrett listened to lies told him by certain rivals of Alexis's in the music department (Bannon, an aging

51

fop, professor of composition, is especially jealous of Alexis), or by people like Gowan Vaughan-Jones or Warren Hochberg, who have never quite managed to disguise their loathing of Alexis—pedantic bastards forever talking of scholarly "standards" at Woodslee, self-appointed fag haters—or perhaps it was Roger Haas, the university's chief attorney, or Brigit Stott, who stared at him so rudely a few minutes ago—as if that bitch hasn't acquired quite a legendary reputation herself—or Lewis Seidel, despite his forced display of admiration for Alexis's work ("I played your sinfonietta the other evening—dusted the record off and played it for some students who had dropped in—and it's really quite good, Alexis, it's still *alive*—a pity it seems to have disappeared from sight—") and his even more forced display of casual camaraderie—or perhaps it was that fantastical cow Mrs. Garrett, all bifocals and wispy bangs and cruel hard joyless grandmother smiles, listening greedily to gossip told her by faculty wives. Ryerson called in Alexis one dismal winter afternoon and told him it might be a good idea for him to cast about for another position; he had been very embarrassed and seemed genuinely stricken. He *seemed* concerned for Alexis's position. But refused to explain the issue, who had complained about Alexis or brought charges against him, who wanted him to leave Woodslee and who wanted him to stay.... Alexis's hysterics alarmed Ryerson but he did not explain, and though the issue blew over, after several weeks of the sort Alexis hopes not to endure again, during which he was drunk much of the time and too sick to meet classes, there is the distinct possibility that his enemies will strike again....

All this is stirring, exciting. In a strange way invigorating.

Is he playing for his enemies tonight? At this very moment?

And for Albert St. Dennis, at last.

The piece is difficult, quite tricky; a virtuoso piece; showy in a subdued way. Not very long. His own composition of some years back, written out in Aspen, not yet recorded but admired by several pianists of his acquaintance: echoes of Cowell, Cowell of the twenties, and echoes of Ives. A tiny heartbeat of a moment lifted—lifted playfully and with gratitude—from *Thoreau*. But the work is Alexis's, all Alexis's, and no one else's. Tone clusters, outrageous percussive hammerings, and then a teardrop of a break, and a moment of silence, and on, on, into the powerful last section.... They are listening. They are being forced to listen. Marilyn Byrne claims to have had the piano tuned just that morning, hoping Alexis will play, and Oliver Byrne is standing just a few feet away, absorbed, watching the incredible feats of Alexis's hands. Does he really admire Alexis, is he really as supportive of Alexis as he appears to be...? Arguing in the university senate that more money must be allotted to the fine arts program, that the university match the state's grant for a Woodslee Center for the Performing Arts...not afraid to speak of his hope to make Woodslee a true community of artists, scholars, teachers, and humanists.... He hired Alexis some years ago, against the wishes of other administrators and, certainly, against the wishes of most members of the music department, and he has supported him since, though he would not tell Alexis the details of the attempted purge last winter. He does not *tell* anyone anything; beneath his social manner he is taciturn, perhaps even secretive. Balding but handsome, always nicely dressed, something military about his bearing but a lover of culture, rumored to play the piano himself and to have been an amateur actor before coming to Woodslee—rumored, even, to write poetry— Byrne is an exceptional administrator and one of the few people at Woodslee whom Alexis admires. But his wife, that perennial Girl Scout—! Thick ankles, over-earnest smiles, totally unconvincing in her "interest" in Alexis.... Perhaps Mrs. Byrne is one of Alexis's enemies: it wouldn't surprise him in the slightest.

It was through Byrne that Alexis made contact with Albert St. Dennis last spring, and through Byrne that Alexis received a small, token grant from the University Arts Council to enable him to take a semester off from teaching and to compose a cycle of songs based on St. Dennis's *Lovesounds*—those remarkable, chilling sonnets of the thirties. Alexis had come across the poems some years before and had been struck, at the time, by their resemblance to a certain kind of music—sly, coy, and yet melancholy—the word-sounds eerily musical—haunting—the sort of music he sometimes heard in his own head but could not quite transpose into notes. The words, disguised as bearers of meaning, were, in fact, ingeniously arranged constructs of sound. Alexis had read them aloud. He would write a musical accompaniment—he *must* do something with the sonnets—must translate them into his own art: otherwise they would be lost to him. But years passed, other works intervened, his life went ragged and frail and he came close to dying (or so he realized afterward: at the time he had existed in a kind of trance, detached from his own actions and his own physical pain), and the sonnets were temporarily forgotten. Then, last fall, he came upon them again, by accident; and not a week later he heard that Dean Byrne was trying to get Albert St. Dennis to come to Woodslee for a year—one of those remarkable coincidences, the sort that seem to occur in Alexis's life at regular intervals. He is not crudely superstitious but these things *do* happen. (Just as "Albert" and "Alexis" resemble each other, and even "St. Dennis" and "Kessler" have some of the same sounds.) So Alexis had run over to Byrne's office and spoken excitedly to him about the project—allowing Byrne to know, or to assume, that the song cycle was already begun—wasn't that a marvelous coincidence?—and that he would like very much to write to St. Dennis himself, to urge him to come here, and of course to ask formal permission for use of the poems, which he had not yet done. Byrne had seemed pleased. He too believed it was something of a coincidence.

Hurriedly, Alexis had put together a package of materials for St. Dennis: a cassette of certain pieces of his, and some photostated reviews of his work, and a photograph taken when he was about twenty-seven. (He is now thirty-two, though he looks, of course, a decade younger.) And a lengthy, handwritten letter, in which he spoke quite nakedly of his deep admiration for St. Dennis's work, especially *Lovesounds*. That cycle of hallucination, pain, despair, ecstasy—and recovery! St. Dennis was, Alexis claimed, a genius in his poetry, his art, but a genius, as well, in his life. For how many people knew what he seemed to know...? How many had survived the sort of catastrophe he described, from the inside, in that sonnet sequence...? The letter had been fifteen pages long. Alexis had written it late one night in a kind of delirium, tears in his eyes, his lips moving silently. The poetry was so beautiful, so powerful—it demanded to be translated into music—it *must* be metamorphosed into Alexis's art. The project meant so very, very much to him. It was all he cared to work on in this phase of his life. If St. Dennis would be kind enough to give him permission, he would be grateful the rest of his life. He would never forget St. Dennis's generosity. And the song cycle would be his gift to St. Dennis, one artist's homage to another.

I am entering a period of rebirth, Alexis thought.

I am not finished with my life after all. So he thought.

So he thought then, last spring, and so he thinks now, as he plays his *Vivace* for St. Dennis and the others, hair in his face, perspiration running down his sides. They are listening: they are being carried along by the music, by his music, by him. How can they resist? He knows the piece is exquisite, he knows he is playing as well as ever. No matter what the condition of his nerves, Alexis is capable—usually—of playing the piano well. He began, after all, as a small child. One and two hours a day, and then three, four, five....At the height of his obsession with this particular instrument he was practicing (though he did not call it "practicing" to himself) between eight and ten hours a day. The power in his fingers—! The joy of the music itself, of music regardless of its emotional tone—! It is the *fact* of art that matters, not the art itself, not, surely, the message or the theme or the effect it has upon others. Mystery. Magic. The one incontestable good. Never-failing beauty of art, of music, no matter who creates it or performs it, no matter what they think of him—staring at his back as if they wish to see into his skull, into his very soul—cagey with him, disapproving of his life (though they know nothing of his life—his "private" life) and even of his physical appearance. Never-failing beauty: the cascade of notes, the stubborn crystal-bright clusters of sound, pricking, painful, gliding, hammering, liquid, fluttering, serene, cataclysmic....Is St. Dennis listening? He remained seated in his chair; he didn't get to his feet as a few of the others did, to gather nearer the piano. Of course he is an old man. Not very well, it seems. And rather drunk.

Alexis hears his music as if it were somewhat detached from him, a miracle that springs from his fingertips, and yet is clear of him, uncontaminated by him. He is—he knows—not the person he had wished to be. There is—he knows at such times, when he is deep in his music—something wrong: something wrong. But what...? Why...? How...? He knows, he knows. He cannot say. Wordless sounds assail him. The music springs from him, streams through him, uses him to find its way into the world, and it does not matter that he is Alexis Kessler—flawed, failed, aging, doomed, spiteful, childish, in debt—most of all in debt—it does not matter who he is: only the music matters. That is his triumph.

But the music moves so quickly!

The evening has moved so quickly!

Tonight, introduced to St. Dennis, he had squeezed the old man's hand and smiled his dazzling hopeful smile and recieved, in return, a rather puzzled half-smile.... "We know each other, we've been corresponding," Alexis said, still smiling. St. Dennis glanced at Marilyn Byrne, as if appealing for help; Marilyn, jumpier than usual, stammered something about "composer-in-residence" but failed to say that her husband had put Alexis in contact with St. Dennis and that Alexis was the young man working on a song cycle based on St. Dennis's sonnets. Alexis was forced to explain, himself, and it seemed to him that St. Dennis recalled the project...it *seemed* the old man had caught on.... He recognized Alexis, that was certain. Recognized his face. *That* was certain.

He had been surprisingly rude to a few of the other guests—barking and jeering and more or less shouting them down—but quite charming to Alexis, though he said little. His glances were friendly, even rather paternal. He *did* recognize Alexis.... Of course he arrived at the Byrnes' fairly drunk; that had been something of a surprise. Alexis had heard the old man was a vegetarian and a non-drinker. Or was that another distinguished English poet? No matter, no matter. Albert St. Dennis has come to Woodslee, to Alexis Kessler, he is here tonight, a man of genius, in this very room, tonight, not far away, listening, absorbed in Alexis's music....

A stir? Something wrong? Alexis does not hear; he will not hear. The piece is nearly ended. He is hunched over the keyboard, his strong, perfect fingers in control. Nothing has gone wrong. He has never played more beautifully. Making love does not demand of Alexis such exquisite control, such deep affection, such respect.... Making love is something technical, a mere skill, at best a kind of talent; making music is something impossible to fathom. The one is a diversion, the other is life itself.

He is very warm, flushed, transported out of himself: yet detached. The music is impersonal in its beauty. It insists upon its own motion, it shapes itself, flowing through him, accelerating his heartbeat—

What is wrong? Is something wrong?

The piece is nearly ended—

But there is something wrong, a commotion, a muttering in the room. Alexis stops playing. His fingers stop. He turns on the piano bench, shaking his hair out of his eyes, astonished, his face burning—How *dare* anyone disturb his playing?—

A sudden gagging sound. It is St. Dennis. On his feet now, at the other end of the living room, the old man seems to be in distress. Brigit Stott is beside him, her arm linked through his. "Mr. St. Dennis!" she cries in a throaty, incredulous voice, "why—what's wrong? What's wrong?" He staggers, his knees buckle, the poor woman is practically holding him up. While everyone stares he stoops over suddenly and begins to vomit. Marilyn Byrne cries something unintelligible, a shout of sheer angry despair—and in the next instant presses

57

her hand over her mouth. But no one has heard: all are staring at Albert St. Dennis. Something light-colored and liquid flows from him, splattering his vest and trousers, splashing onto the Byrnes' handsome Oriental carpet. He gags and chokes and retches, helpless, bent nearly double.

My God, my God, Alexis thinks, his hands still poised over the keyboard, *this cannot be.*

But it is, it happens, it will not be undone.

The Byrnes' party is ending abruptly.

By Monday—no, even by Sunday—people will have spread the word, laughing richly at Alexis Kessler's humiliation. He can imagine their sneers, their satisfied grins. Albert St. Dennis was sick to his stomach listening to a piano sonata of Kessler's! Yes! Yes, really! *Yes.* In full view of the Byrnes' guests. It will be reported in the Phoenix Heights area by the Haases and perhaps by Marilyn Byrne herself, and up on the Old Armory Road by the Hochbergs, and along the Valley Mills Drive by the Housleys, and around campus by Gowan Vaughan-Jones and Brigit Stott and Gladys Fetler, and in the residential area just east of the university, where everyone lives, by the Seidels and the Tomlinsons and the Ryersons and the others, the young couples whose names Alexis has forgotten—and by Wednesday the entire university community will know about it. Alexis writhes in despair, thinking of it. Another Kessler tale! Another Kessler defeat! His enemies will gloat, his rivals will repeat the story and embellish it, even his friendly acquaintances will spread it across town and back. When police raided an apartment two floors down from Alexis's last autumn and arrested several people on marijuana charges—which were later dropped—the story leaped across Woodslee that Alexis Kessler had been arrested, that he was in jail along with a number of other drug users, that he would certainly be fired from Woodslee. In some versions of the story Alexis was dragged out by police naked except for his jewelry; in other versions, he was completely unconscious and had to be carried out. Some said that his bail was set so high—$100,000—that he had had to telephone numerous relatives and old friends to raise bond. Some said the judge refused to let him go at all. A corruptor of youth! A degenerate!...While the stories wound their way through the university community, becoming ever more outlandish and artistic, colliding with one another, sometimes joining one another, Alexis was forced to meet with his classes as usual, and with his colleagues, who eyed him with great interest but never mentioned the scandal. And so it went....And the stories were never exactly refuted, because they were not public and not available to Alexis. It simply happened that they reached a peak and then declined and faded and disappeared, to be resurrected when another "Kessler" scandal came along.

What good does it do, Alexis thinks dully, St. Dennis apologizing now so passionately...? The old man is so sorry, so very sorry. Clutching at Alexis's arm. Practically weeping. (He, too, is worried about his reputation, Alexis suddenly realizes. St. Dennis, of all people!) What good does it do, this expression of regret? Too late. The party is ending, the party is over, most of the guests have escaped. Only midnight and the party is over.

"I...I...I simply can't express, Mr. Alexander, how ashamed I am," St. Dennis says, leaning toward Alexis, his head thrust forward in a way that is both cringing and aggressive. "How very, very sorry....Simply can't think what happened, what seemed to...suddenly... come over me."

"That's all right," Alexis mutters.

"I was enjoying the music so much," St. Dennis says eagerly, "I was sitting with my eyes closed and listening, utterly transported...utterly charmed...Wasn't I, Mrs. Stott? Weren't we both? Such a very, very fine...such a very fine little concert....Simply can't think what happened to me," he says, shaking his head slowly. "I do hope you will accept my apology."

"Fine," Alexis says.

"...And Mrs. Byrne, your rug! What a shame!"

"No, no," Marilyn says at once, "it's nothing, really; really nothing. It's already cleaned up—you see? Nothing to it! The stain will disappear by tomorrow."

"I hope you'll send me the bill if—"

"Mr. St. Dennis, please, there's no need to apologize, there's no need at all," Marilyn says warmly. "We're more concerned about *you*. We only want you to be happy here. Don't we, Oliver? I think that—all the excitement—"

"Yes, the excitement—the turmoil—The shock of landing on this planet," St. Dennis says vaguely, trying to smile, "I mean this continent—among strangers—I mean, among—among—The strangeness of it, don't you see, the heady excitement of—a new life—new vistas and adventures—Simply too much for my shaky old system."

"No, Mr. St. Dennis, no, really, it's just the late hour—"

"I behaved inexcusably," he says, touching Alexis's shoulder, turning to Brigit Stott and smiling sadly. "I wonder if these two young people will ever forgive me...."

He reaches out for Brigit Stott's hand; he grasps it firmly in his own. Alexis feels, for an instant, a prick of jealousy.

The Stott woman looks surprisingly attractive, as if given a kind of perverse energy by St. Dennis's distress. Woodslee is sharply divided on the subject of Brigit Stott's charm: a number of people find her strangely appealing, even rather beautiful in a soiled, depraved way, and others—the majority—find her very odd indeed. The rumors of her promiscuity! Her desperation! Her drinking! The mess of her apartment, where she lives with five or six cats—the ugly tales that circulate freely about her behavior during her marriage—her cruelty to students and to friends—her habit of forgetting people entirely, simply erasing them from her consideration. A vicious woman, Alexis has heard. Supremely self-contained, egotistical. Eccentric. Doesn't she carry a revolver in her purse, or at least a knife—? Tonight her eyes are ringed with fatigue and her unfashionable dark lipstick is partly eaten off and she seems vulnerable, very human. Not at all formidable. Her graying hair has gone limp; there are several large stains on the skirt of her severe black dress—stains from St. Dennis's vomit, most likely. She is saying something about St. Dennis having been no trouble at all—he shouldn't be distressed—not at all. Everyone assents. But St. Dennis continues to squeeze her hand, staring at her. Alexis is suddenly quite annoyed.

He makes an impatient move, as if to leave; and St. Dennis looks around at once and takes his arm. "And you, my boy, you most of all—I've offended you irreparably, haven't I—Mr. Alexander, is it? Is that your name?"

"It doesn't matter," Alexis says at once. But his voice is raw and young and hurt. There is a childish whine in it that alarms him.

Someone tells St. Dennis Alexis's name and St. Dennis nods slowly, blinking. The name must mean nothing to him. Old fool! Drunk! Once a genius, no doubt, but now a doddering ruin; not even a very intriguing ruin. Alexis would push past these boring people and escape, but St. Dennis is holding his arm. . . . He had missed his chance for a dramatic exit some time ago: when his sonata was so rudely and stupidly interrupted, he should have risen from the piano bench with no sign of the outrage he felt (for signs of emotional weakness are taken up at once by one's detractors), he should simply have walked out of the Byrnes' house and into the night. His apartment building is a considerable distance away but a hard, brisk, self-punishing walk would do him good. Now it is too late.

Everyone is offering to drive Albert St. Dennis home.

Lewis Seidel is the most aggressive; he has his car keys out and is rattling them. Alexis can see that St. Dennis's interest in Brigit Stott and in himself has annoyed Seidel. "It *is* late for Mr. St. Dennis, who isn't used to our way of life yet," Seidel says. "Faye and I will be only too happy to drive you home, Mr. St. Dennis. Shall we go—?"

"Yes, I think that—If—"

Oliver Byrne interrupts. "I had thought I might drive Mr. St. Dennis home myself. Isn't it out of your way, Lewis?"

"Out of my way? In what sense?" Seidel says, staring. He and Byrne contemplate each other. Alexis recalls a rumor he had heard a while back—that Seidel wants Byrne displaced as dean, that he wants the position for himself, that he and several other powerful members of the faculty are planning a move to "dethrone" Byrne this fall. The two men had seemed friendly enough tonight, in Alexis's opinion, and of course the wives seemed friendly—Faye was always "friendly" and Marilyn really had no choice—but now it appears they are not on good terms at all. Seidel can hardly manage his characteristic insouciance, his wide-eyed frank sincerity, and Oliver Byrne, unusually pale, can hardly control his voice, which trembles slightly when he is upset. "...You know very well that Faye and I live on Strathmore, and Mr. St. Dennis's apartment building is right out on Phoenix Boulevard. Isn't it? Right on our way home," Seidel says gaily. "And even if it weren't— would *that* matter? Mr. St. Dennis's comfort comes first."

"Thank you," St. Dennis whispers. "I think that—"

"It's still quite early," Byrne says weakly.

But he has lost, the party is over and he has lost, it's hardly midnight and the evening has come to an abrupt end. Marilyn Byrne looks drained and disappointed; her forehead and nose are shining, her smile is unconvincing, her upright, self-conscious posture seems ludicrous and strained. Poor woman! Alexis feels sorry for her. Oliver Byrne, usually so confident, usually so much in control, looks boyish in defeat—rubbing his hands together—trying to regain his magistral smile. St. Dennis was *his* accomplishment, his *coup*. Everyone has been saying of him that he has done an excellent job as Dean of Humanities—a truly superb job—and for months people have congratulated him on the acquisition of Albert St. Dennis. Now he must surrender him to Lewis Seidel. And the old man's grayish, deathly look isn't very encouraging.

"If you'd like to spend the night with us, Mr. St. Dennis," Byrne says, "we do have a guest room—in fact we have two—and—I mean, if you're feeling unwell— It would be no trouble—"

But this suggestion is absurd, and no one takes him up on it.

"Thank you for a fine, fine evening," St. Dennis says weakly, "but now I really must say good night. *Enough?— too much!* As this lovely young woman has said. You understand, I hope—?"

It happens that Alexis and Brigit Stott are swept along with St. Dennis, squeezed into the back seat of the Seidels' car; St. Dennis will not surrender them. Alexis protests that he can walk home—he would really prefer to walk home—and Brigit says, in her hoarse, almost inaudible voice, that she could very easily call a cab. But St. Dennis grips each by the arm and holds them fast and has assumed, now, an odd sly grandfatherly air, a rakish, conspiratorial manner. "Thank God for fresh air! Thank God for freedom! American hospitality—it's really quite amazing, isn't it?" he murmurs. The three of them squeeze into the back seat of the Siedels' car though Alexis knows very well that Lewis doesn't want him, and probably doesn't even want Brigit; he wants St. Dennis to himself.

Phoenix Heights, where the Byrnes live, is only a fifteen-minute drive from the university area, where an apartment has been rented for St. Dennis in a handsome old building; during this drive Lewis Seidel tries to ask St. Dennis a few questions, glancing into the rear-view mirror, but the old man ignores him, chatting away companionably with Alexis and Brigit, their hands in his. Somehow he has gotten onto the subject of Auden: an old rival, no longer in the competition, whose lust for the Nobel Prize was legendary. Did they know? Did they *know* the degree of the poor man's craving? It was, St. Dennis says with relish, positively embarrassing.

Alexis says he doesn't know—mumbles that he knows very little about poets.

Brigit says she had heard Auden was quite a kind, generous man; but of course he had had a drinking problem....

St. Dennis ignores her remark and for the rest of the drive talks of Auden's undeniable but limited gift, the folly of his personal life, the fact that the poor man had been nowhere near the Nobel Prize—how deluded he had been! Alas! How deluded so many of them were, St. Dennis's contemporaries! And so many of them had fallen by the wayside, it was really quite pitiful, quite...frightening. He names names, mumbling, sniffing. Alexis doesn't recognize most of the names. He glances over at Brigit Stott, who is looking at him. An alarmed smile? A conspiratorial smile? Poor old St. Dennis is muttering and sniffing loudly and he seems unaware of his surroundings, his eyes half shut, his jowls sagging, lips loose and damp. Auden and folly and the vanity of human wishes and the litany of the dead, the poor pathetic helpless dead, the world filling up with them, being appropriated by them, the earth and the air and the streams, the dwelling places of the dead, the Mothers and Fathers, the Hosts, Yeats knew, Auden knew, St. Dennis knows, he can smell them and taste them, hadn't he written of the plunge of life in *The Explorers*, which must, alas, lose its energy and its sacred, proud beauty and come to rest...come to rest as the Explorer-heroes came to rest, ultimately, in the arms of the Mothers...hadn't he written of it already ...must he live it out now in the flesh? "My dears, you've been too kind to me," he says, his voice broken and tearful. "I don't deserve it. You...you...you are so young and beautiful...your love is so pure...so...so frightening to an old man.... *The young in one another's arms:* ah yes! Yes! *That!* It's true. Am I bitter? Are any of us bitter, old men poets, shaking our bones? I think...yes...I think we are bitter but we are also...we are also...we...also.... We celebrate, don't you see, the plunge...the love...the young lovers.... Not jealous. Not. Envy maybe. Quite natural, isn't it. And so I...I...I want you only to be happy," he says, beginning to weep.

And then he does an incredible thing: he brings Alexis's and Brigit's hands together, squeezes them together on his knees. And they cannot resist. Staring at each other over the old man's sagging head, they exchange a look of sheer stupefaction. It is a moment they will remember all their lives. "...happy. Lovers. The young. The eternally young. In each other's arms.... And

no bitterness. None. Only celebration. Poetry and celebration and...."

That occurs at 12:20 A.M. By 1:45 A.M. Brigit Stott and
Alexis Kessler *have* become lovers. In a sense.

The Seidels drive Albert St. Dennis home, across the river and south into the small city of Woodslee; the drive would be pleasant—there is a glaring half-moon in the sky, the river is dark and placid and lovely, Lewis inhales the fresh, chilly air in noisy gulps and proclaims it a tonic, a life-saver (he has been coughing much of the evening, a dry wracking painful cough)—except for the fact that Lewis can't interrupt the old man's babbling to ask him certain important questions. He glances at St. Dennis in the rear-view mirror, noting grimly the tear streaks on the old man's cheeks. Unbelievable. Drunken sentimental babbling. Perhaps what he says is valuable—Lewis can make out important words now and then, like "Auden," "death," "art," "fate," "Nobel Prize"—but it is an incoherent jumble, a terrible disappointment.

Lewis has been planning for months a highly original kind of critical work: by no means ordinary criticism, and not even speculative, experimental metacriticism of the sort being done by younger men who are scornful of old-fashioned structures and value judgments; but a dialogue, a duet, his own voice and that of a representative artist of the old order, locked together in ferocious combat. The artist is to be, of course, Albert St. Dennis. Lewis has read all his books, even the early, minor works and the embarrassingly bad propaganda prose poems of the thirties; he has always been a voracious reader, a tireless seeker of truth. As a young man at CCNY he had, for a while, spent so many hours in the library that his vision had begun to be affected; the strain had been so great he had thought he might go mad, his eyesight violated by tiny darting black specks that swelled and faded and reappeared whimsically. The most devastating attack had taken place while Lewis was plowing through Marx. He had actually whimpered aloud and rushed from his carrel in the library and out into the street, clutching at his head.... But he was, even then, a highly charged and aggressive person with no respect for weakness, not even his own, and so he had forced himself back to his books, eyestrain or not, headache and dizziness and fears of madness notwithstanding, and he had conquered Marx to his own satisfaction, as he had conquered, one by one, book by book, every important writer of the modern era. It had been necessary for him to abandon his early, boyish enthusiasm for books, for "liking" and "enjoying" were outmoded means of approaching literature; but in place of such simple-minded enthusiasm Lewis learned to experience the far more complex satisfactions of the scholar-critic who not only comprehends his material but, in a sense, overcomes it.

And so he has read all of St. Dennis's books; he even owns most of them, having ordered them this summer from various booksellers, in preparation for St. Dennis's residency at Woodslee and for his dialogue with him. A Nietzschean duet, a contest of sorts, the "old" and the "new" struggling together, so that out of their fierce death-combat a timeless truth might emerge. Of course the essay—or perhaps it will be a book, with wide margins and experimental typography—will be totally original, possibly not even about poetry at all, but about ways of perceiving reality. So-called "reality," that is: for Lewis knows very well that reality doesn't exist, not as the simple-minded nineteenth-century thinkers (Marx, for one) believed. A highly provocative, outrageous, stunningly original, baffling, exasperating, but brilliant contribution to literary thought.... *A highly provocative, challenging, sometimes outrageous and sometimes beautifully clear work...goes beyond even Seidel's earlier books....A highly provocative, original mind, a critic who is really a poet himself....Criticism is, perhaps, the highest art form; in reading the brilliant, provocative works of Lewis Seidel, one is continually forced to consider this odd, rather alarming proposition....*

Dialogues evidently grew out of a historic series of confrontations between Lewis Seidel and the distinguished poet Albert St. Dennis (whom the dust jacket described as "close, loyal, affectionate friends") but it is, in this reviewer's opinion, a work that goes far beyond any ordinary debate as we know it. Seidel's most recent book, the highly controversial Cul-de-sac *of 1959, a close study of the philosophical assumptions of Henry James's fiction, brilliant as it was, did not prepare us for the stunning originality of* Dialogues....*A new form of criticism, iconoclastic and merciless and certain to be widely imitated by young critics everywhere: in every way a masterful creation.*

But: St. Dennis is merely babbling. And all evening he managed to avoid Lewis, as if he had taken, from the first, an irrational dislike to him. (And his rudeness to poor Faye—quite incomprehensible.) Of course Lewis has a great deal of time. Months. St. Dennis is certain to be impressed, when sober, by the fact that Lewis is the only person at Woodslee (with the possible exception of Gowan Vaughan-Jones, who is working on an immense study of twentieth-century poetics that will include a chapter on St. Dennis and his imitators) to have read all his books, *all* his books; he is certainly the only person at Woodslee to own these books. That, surely, will impress the old man.... Lewis has already told Faye they will have St. Dennis over for dinner as soon as possible, so he can show St. Dennis the books and ask him to inscribe them; and they will have the next big party for him, scheduled to follow his first public address in November. (The Hochbergs wanted to have this party but Lewis argued Warren out of it, claiming that the Hochbergs' house—some nine or ten miles north of the city—was simply too far for St. Dennis to go immediately after his lecture on campus; it was more reasonable, wasn't it, for the Seidels to be hosts, since they lived only five minutes from the university...?) As time passes it seems quite likely that Lewis and St. Dennis will become friends, intimate friends, despite the disparity in their ages. (Lewis is now fifty-one, but looks no more than forty-five.) The Seidels' home on Strathmore is hardly three blocks from St. Dennis's apartment, and since the old man hasn't a car, and won't know his way around, it is altogether probable that Lewis will drive him to parties this winter; the old man might want to go to New York, to visit his publishers, or to Boston, and Lewis could drive him there, and meet St. Dennis's friends, and perhaps introduce St. Dennis to friends and acquaintances of his own; a former student of Lewis's, a beautiful girl now working at *Time-Life* and living in the East Village, often invites Lewis to her apartment when he is in the city, and has marvelous, rather crazy parties that last for days at a time...it might be educational for old St. Dennis to be exposed to such people. Lewis will be a close observer, noting the old man's reactions, memorizing his remarks—which are certain to be sharper and more original than those he has uttered this evening....After the year is over and St. Dennis returns to London, it is quite likely that Lewis will be a regular guest at his Chelsea apartment, or flat, and that St. Dennis will introduce Lewis Seidel to the London literary world. (None of his books, thus far, have been published in England, a phenomenon utterly baffling to Lewis and to his New York publisher and to his many admirers in the United States.) Perhaps St. Dennis's next book of poems will be dedicated to Lewis Seidel, "the American Socrates"...or "the American Nietzsche"....No: simply "my American friend." A slim volume, the poet's last work; possibly a posthumous work. Lewis will fly to England for the funeral. Lewis ("the only person of my acquaintance to have not only bought all my books but to have actually read them") might even be mentioned in the old man's will. The *New York Times* might quote...might photograph....The *Times Literary Supplement*....*Time* and *Newsweek* and....A photograph of the two men together, taken (perhaps) at Woodslee, during the poet's residence there. Taken at the Seidels' house, perhaps. St. Dennis and Seidel. (Must have the Polaroid on hand for that party; but mustn't be too obvious about it. Faye could introduce, maybe. Midparty. Spontaneous.) And then, after a decent period of time, Lewis's memoirs of the grand old man will appear....

Excited, Lewis glances in the rear-view mirror and

asks St. Dennis if the night air has refreshed him a little, if he feels better?—but the old man doesn't hear. He repeats his question; but the old man doesn't hear. Faye whispers to him not to drive so fast; he's over the white line, hasn't he noticed—? Lewis ignores her. He sees that Brigit Stott and Alexis Kessler are sitting close beside St. Dennis, their heads inclined toward his; opportunists, bitchy and pragmatic and ruthless, both of them...why did Byrne invite them to his party? The Stott woman had to be invited, perhaps, since she is in the English department and is a writer, the department's only novelist, but the Kessler creature makes no sense at all, no sense at all. A homosexual, flagrant and malicious and arrogant, attractive enough, no doubt, in a superficial way, but surely not fit company for Albert St. Dennis. It might be that the Byrnes are simply naive...? Or is Oliver coldly and shrewdly scheming his way to the presidency by means of an odd assortment of people and events and interlocking relationships Lewis cannot hope to figure out...? It is no secret that Byrne wants to be president of Woodslee; Garrett himself knows that, and though in public he seems to support Byrne, in private, it is said, he detests the man. (Byrne was an ambitious young dean at Swarthmore before being brought to Woodslee—that is, bought by Woodslee—some years before, when the university's reputation was at its lowest in seven decades; even Lewis has to admit that Byrne has done an excellent job, has scooped up foundation money and grants from the state legislature and loans for building purposes and promises of still more money, has defended the faculty's stand on tenure, merit raises, and annual salary increments based on cost-of-living scales, is crusading for a new graduate library, and for an expanded center for the performing arts, and for.... He has done an excellent job, so far: even Lewis has to admit that. And the *coup* of St. Dennis is certainly an enviable one. (It was known that Cornell and the University of Texas were both high bidders for St. Dennis, but that Woodslee came through not only because of the amount of money offered but because of the young dean's persuasive personality: he had flown to London twice to talk with St. Dennis.) But the year is only beginning and there are enormous issues ahead, and Lewis is rather skeptical about Byrne's idealism, and not at all "hopeful"—as he has said to innumerable colleagues and to President Garrett himself—about Byrne's continued presence at Woodslee.... Is it possible that Byrne actually *likes* Kessler? And Brigit Stott? Lewis cannot believe that: it's too absurd.

He and Brigit have known each other for three years now, and Lewis had met her earlier in New York City, at about the time her second novel came out and her marriage began to deteriorate. He had liked her well enough at first. She was so painfully shy, almost mute at times, overwhelmed by large parties...really an attractive woman, though too thin for Lewis's taste...and curiously delicate, vulnerable...feminine. Her husband Stanley Fifield, a man of Lewis's size, swarthy-skinned, with a mustache and a quick busy joky manner and stylish clothes, had been very protective of her; Lewis remembers a party on New York's West Side in someone's big apartment where Fifield more or less blocked guests from approaching his wife, who stood in a corner sipping a drink nervously, her black hair down to her shoulders at that time, glossy and much thicker than it is now, and not yet streaked with gray...he remembers slipping around Fifield and approaching Brigit with a wide, hearty grin and a handshake, telling the frightened woman that he had read both her novels and liked them very, very much and that he thought she was the most promising young stylist of.... And then Fifield had interrupted, with the sort of large loose goodhearted manner Lewis himself had perfected.

Yes, Lewis had liked Brigit Stott well enough at that time. He approved of shy, demure, fastidious women, though he tended to be attracted—violently—to tall fleshy extroverted girls, of whom there were many at Woodslee; and he had been the one who pushed Brigit's appointment here, arguing Warren Hochberg out of his choice of an older, far more conventional woman writer, a New England regionalist whose husband was related in some tedious, complicated way to Vivian Hochberg. (The department had had to hire a woman that year, at all costs: Gladys Fetler was their only woman professor,

71

and though she was a full professor whose salary was nearly at the top of the scale, her appointment had been made in 1942 and there had not been another permanent appointment of a woman since; the State Commission on Woman's Rights was investigating Woodslee, and a federal agency was planning to block loans to a number of universities and institutions that did not comply with certain guidelines on the hiring of women and minorities. "Outrageous sexism," someone had charged.) So Stott was hired and the commission got off their backs.

Is she one of your former girls? colleagues asked, winking.

Certainly not, Lewis said.

Come on, now, Lewis!—we won't tell our wives, and our wives won't tell *your* wife. The woman's name is Brigit Stott and she's a young novelist and you can vouch for her work, and for her ability to get along with students, and—?

Brigit and I are only friends, Lewis said. Old, good friends.

"Friends"—?

And she isn't all that young, actually, Lewis said with a touch of regret.

But though he insisted they had never been lovers, and had not even slept together—Lewis used the expression "slept together" out of a real disdain for more contemporary slang, which his students, even his girl students, used quite casually—his colleagues at Woodslee nevertheless believed there was something between the two of them, some shared experience, some secret, perhaps even a mutual contempt for the faculty at Woodslee and for the faculty wives. Your Brigit Stott is quite an interesting woman, they might say, with a faint emphasis upon the *your*. Your friend Brigit has turned out to be rather eccentric in certain ways, hasn't she?—though the students seem unusually enthusiastic about her lectures. What is her candid opinion of us, has she told you?

It was difficult for Lewis to resist—indeed, he found himself unable to resist—hinting that, yes, Brigit Stott did confide in him occasionally; and yes, they had been friends, quite intimate friends, years before in New

72

York. But privately he was disappointed in her. Disappointed and distressed and hurt and bewildered.

Betrayed, really.

From the very first she has shown little interest in Lewis; she seems to have no time for him, no awareness of the importance of his ideas in relationship to the art of prose fiction. She could learn a great deal from him, but she resists; and she is not nearly so shy as Lewis had believed. (She has declined several of Faye's invitations to dinner over the years, though she usually accepts invitations to larger parties.) Lewis loves to talk, to argue, to harangue; he is the department's most popular undergraduate teacher, and his students crowd around him after class and in the coffee shop and at the Riverview, a tavern near the university, eager to hear his ideas. Certain of his colleagues are very respectful also; tonight at the Byrnes' those two young assistant professors, Jaeger and Swanson, Ernest Jaeger and Barry Swanson, were fascinated by his remarks on Borges and Barthes and Kafka...their wives, too, had been deeply absorbed in his argument. Mrs. Garrett claims to be an admirer of his; she sometimes audits his course in the American novel, sitting at the rear of the little amphitheater and taking notes like any student, coloring slightly at Lewis's ribald jokes—for he *is* outspoken, and often shocking; that is the Seidel manner. Other faculty wives attend his lectures from time to time. And he still receives compliments on *Cul-de-sac*, and invitations from universities to give lectures or attend conferences (he is a very successful speaker, in fact, once he manipulates his audience into laughter), and he is engaged in correspondence with nearly one hundred writers, critics, and scholars everywhere in the world, including Japan and New Zealand and Nigeria and Pakistan. His archives will be a treasure. It seems to him, at times, that he is taken very seriously by everyone except Brigit Stott—who, more than most, should be grateful to him, and respectful of his work. Her attitude bewilders him, and angers him, for isn't it a kind of provocation...? Doesn't she know how powerful he is...?

(Still, he is wary of her: for it is generally known in Woodslee that Brigit Stott is working on an immense roman à clef in which all of Woodslee figures—a merciless, venomous satire that might very well destroy careers and lives and provoke—so the rumors hint—a number of libel suits.)

Sometimes he likes her, and sometimes he hates her. It is she who is unpredictable—ungovernable. Appearing shy and even tongue-tied, she is capable, nevertheless, of coming out with extraordinary statements, especially when she has had a bit to drink. (The drinking *is* a problem, Lewis has come to believe; Faye has told him some unpleasant tales related to her by other faculty wives about Brigit's behavior.) She once said within earshot of the university's ambitious but sadly limited vice-president Clay Waller—whom everyone more or less scorns—that "lack of power corrupts": and the remark became famous at Woodslee. She cruelly undercut a pedantic discussion by Gowan Vaughan-Jones, of all people, on the subject of the history of the sonnet with a single disparaging remark, and she said of Gladys Fetler's highly respected scholarship that "no one reads it"—though she seems to be genuinely fond of Dr. Fetler and to have meant no harm by the remark or, indeed, by any of the remarks. They seem to leap from her without her conscious knowledge. Perhaps it is the effect of the alcohol on her delicate nervous system...? Her remark tonight about Lewis's ideas was really rather unforgivable. *Sometimes brilliant, sometimes shit.* Yes: really unforgivable.

Though possibly it is the woman's way of flirting with him...?

Not that it mattered in the slightest. Lewis is accustomed to being attacked in public, and he is adroit at turning even the crudest attack to his own advantage. All he requires is an audience! He had seized the issue gladly enough and acquitted himself well, impressing St. Dennis and the others with the range and depth and ferocity of his knowledge, and the rapidity of his mind; so it had turned out well. In a way he was grateful to Brigit for having stimulated him into speech. But she herself had appeared bored, turning a ring round and round her finger, refusing to look at Lewis though it was obvious he was really addressing her and cared very much for her opinion. Instead she has stared at Kessler for a long time until even Kessler, who normally craved attention, grew uneasy. A strange woman, not nearly so feminine as everyone had thought, rather disappointing, rather maddening....

If she isn't careful, Lewis thinks, watching her in the rear-view mirror, he will force her out of Woodslee: it is in his power, after all, to make things so uncomfortable for certain people that they will give up and flee rather than fight. (He had successfully blocked the promotion from associate professor to full professor of a Victorian specialist who had aroused his antagonism over an issue too complicated to recall, and the man finally quit Woodslee and went elsewhere, without ever knowing—not *really* knowing—who was behind his repeated failure to be promoted; and he had eased out a young American literature specialist just the year before, when the man was up for tenure, having presented to the Promotion and Tenure Committee a very persuasive case against the man's ability to do original research. (In fact, Ernest Jaeger is the man's replacement, and he strikes Lewis as very promising indeed.) Along with several other powerful faculty members Lewis was responsible, some time ago, in forcing the old Dean of Humanities into premature retirement—a stubborn, unimaginative man, with a weak background in literature and history and a perverse distrust of "the arts," who had tried personally to destroy Lewis—but Lewis had not foreseen that Oliver Byrne would be the new dean and that he too, in his own way, would prove so unsatisfactory.) And then there was the unfortunate, rather silly Adrian Hogan....It would not be difficult to force Brigit Stott out, if he put his mind to it. That bitch! So cool to poor Faye's attempts at friendship....Though Lewis isn't chairman of the English department he is nearly as powerful as Warren Hochberg, who respects and fears him, knowing how skillful a politician Lewis has become; it was Lewis, after all, who herded Warren into office, during a tumultuous period in the mid-sixties when it looked, at times, as if the entire university were about to fold. Warren and Lewis are friends. In a sense. In a sense they are friends.... Lewis and Vivian are, oddly, friends; or were. In a sense, also. In a very special sense.

But then, it might be argued that everyone in the department is friendly with everyone else, in a sense.

The night air has revived him but Lewis, too, has had more to drink than he can comfortably handle—because of his nerves he always drinks too much at the Byrnes' pretentious gatherings. Now he realizes he has overshot Alexis Kessler's apartment building, that new high-rise on the Powhatan River, and since he wishes to get rid of Kessler, since he does *not* intend to allow St. Dennis to invite Kessler up to his apartment, he stops before Brigit Stott's apartment building on the corner of Strathmore and Linwood and asks if this is all right for both Brigit and Alexis?—pretending he doesn't know that Alexis lives more than a mile away. Alexis agrees quickly, however, and Brigit murmurs thanks, and despite St. Dennis's protestations—what *does* the man see in these two, anyway?—what perverse enchantment have they worked upon the old fool?—they get out of Lewis's car at last and he drives away, thank God.

Turning onto Linwood he glances back and sees the two standing close together near the building's front entrance; they seem to be talking earnestly.... But what have Brigit and Alexis to talk about? They have never seemed very fond of each other.

By the time Lewis parks before St. Dennis's apartment building on Phoenix Boulevard, the old man has somehow managed to light a cigarette. He is still babbling, now about a Russian poet, something about translations, or perhaps it is his own poetry translated into Russian, or a trip he once made to Russia that was evidently disastrous. Lewis and Faye maneuver him out of the back seat of the car; he drops the cigarette; it falls into his lap, then down along his leg, to the floor of the car; Faye, grunting, has to stoop over to retrieve it. St. Dennis is apologetic. He belches, and apologizes again. His fingers brush against Faye's cheeks as if he were blind.

"Who are you? So kind! Kind. Americans so kind. Food and liquor and cars and warmth and beds and money and good teeth and smiles...smiles.... Who are you? Dean?

Good man. Kind. Talking. Too much talking. Kindness. Money. Cars.... Is this where they have lodged me? Do you have a key? Can't see. Glasses dirty. Oh, thank you so much... didn't see that bloody step."

They maneuver him into the foyer and into the elevator and upstairs to the fifth floor, and walk him along the corridor to his apartment, 508, that faces the boulevard and, across the way, the northeastern corner of the Woodslee campus. The apartment is dark; Lewis switches on the lights.

"Thank you," St. Dennis says with dignity, "... Very kind."

"Be careful of the rug," Lewis says, "it's bunched up here...."

"Don't let him fall, Lewis," Faye cries.

"... Very, very kind," St. Dennis mumbles. He has another cigarette in his fingers and is looking from side to side, blindly, as if for a light. "I'll be able to manage now quite nicely. No trouble at all."

"Should we take him into the bedroom?" Faye asks nervously.

"... no trouble at all," St. Dennis says.

His legs buckle suddenly; they maneuver him to a sofa and he falls onto it; he begins to laugh quietly. From somewhere he has produced a box of matches that he holds in one hand, opening it upside-down, so that matches fall onto his lap and the sofa and the floor. "Harriet," he says softly. "Asleep and nobody's to know. Eh? Mum's the word! What you don't know doesn't hurt. Exactly. Cicero. 'Grace of delivery.'... Don't wish to disturb Harriet, you know; best idea, simply sleep here, sofa here, no trouble at all. Very kind of you."

"Should we just leave him here?" Faye whispers. "It doesn't seem right to...."

"Of course we can't leave him here," Lewis says sharply. He glares at his wife: it is the first time he has looked at her in hours. The sight of her—the sad tinted-blond hair, the penciled eyebrows and dainty rouged cheeks and innocuous pearl earrings—annoy him for some reason. She is not so stupid as she appears, and yet she *appears* to be so stupid! Lewis Seidel's wife, of all people. He suspects people talk about their marriage, about Faye, wondering why he married her. She has gained at least thirty pounds since their wedding. Is it to spite him? To humiliate him in the eyes of his rivals? Of course she is a good mother to their three boys, a good housekeeper, a good cook, a good daughter-in-law, a good hostess, not so clever, perhaps, as Marilyn Byrne, or as confident as Vivian Hochberg, but hard-working and tireless and absolutely loyal to Lewis.... He wonders at his sudden anger; the mere sight of her tired, distressed expression makes him want to shout. "Of course we can't leave him here like this. Don't be so damn stupid. He's likely to start a fire, isn't he, in the condition he's in? Stupid cow. Get out of the way."

"No trouble at all now," St. Dennis says sleepily. "'S nearly morning, isn't it? Church bells. Will wake. Harriet must sleep, must rest. No disturbance. Mrs. Byrne? Is it?... Where is my cigarette?"

"You'd better lie down," Lewis says, embarrassed. "You're very tired, Mr. St. Dennis, you've had an arduous day...evening...so much excitement, conversation.... You're far from home, you know.... Yes, just give me that box. Thanks! You don't want a cigarette at this late hour, do you, you're very sleepy, aren't you, yes, for Christ's sake, Faye, get his other shoe, will you?—take it off, please!—don't stand there so damn helpless. Get a blanket or a quilt or something from the bedroom. Hurry up.... No, Mr. St. Dennis, I think I'll take this box of matches with me...you don't really need a cigarette now, do you?...you were coughing earlier this evening...yes, you're very sleepy, yes, that's right, I'm going to put your glasses right here on the table, see, right here, by the sofa, that's right, that's fine, we've got your shoes off and I'll just loosen your tie a little and...and that should do it, that should be enough; are you comfortable? Yes? These old-fashioned sofas are nice and roomy, aren't they?...Okay, here's a blanket, we'll just tuck you in and you'll be quite safe here, as good as in bed, as good as at home, nothing to worry about, see?...you're already asleep, my friend. Already asleep! Fine."

Lewis checks the apartment quickly, poking his head into the bedroom and into the bathroom and into a small
78

cluttered room that is evidently going to be St. Dennis's study. And into the kitchen, a surprisingly large, dreary room with an old-fashioned sink and worn linoleum. Not very attractive, really. The only decent room is the living room, which is rather small; and even in that room the ancient molding at the ceiling is gray with dust and the carpets are faded. A disappointing place. Lewis is annoyed and plans to complain: surely Woodslee University could have housed this distinguished man in better accommodations. Why did Oliver Byrne put him here?... This apartment building is generally considered to be one of the most interesting examples of Greek Revival architecture in the area; it was purchased by the university some years ago, and while Lewis has always admired its facade, its columns and ornamentation and stately, flaring steps, he has never been impressed by its shabbily elegant foyer and its pretensions to style. It might be necessary for him to locate another apartment for poor St. Dennis.... If the man is really disappointed with this place, he might possibly wish to live with the Seidels; they have a roomy, sprawling house, a late-Victorian monstrosity that is the envy of the university community, very nicely fixed up inside, warm and hospitable and attractive... and Lewis would charge nothing, certainly, for St. Dennis's stay.

"He's asleep," Faye whispers.

"He's unconscious," Lewis says.

Without his glasses the old man looks even frailer. His skin appears to be clammy; it is very pale, almost white. Breathing as if with an effort, he makes a wet wheezing noise, and his lips part in a grimace, revealing his false teeth, too white and too even and slightly large for his narrow chin. Poor man! Lewis pities him. On an impulse he touches St. Dennis's forehead as if blessing him, then, stooped over the sleeping man, he brushes back a strand of limp white hair. Sad. He appears to be older than seventy. Could be eighty, at least. Lewis's father is seventy-eight now and in excellent condition, except for his arthritis; St. Dennis looks older. The blanket is drawn up to his chin and tucked in around his shoulders. He sleeps, wheezing, obliterated by the sudden depth of his sleep, the plunge into sleep, its terrible necessity. Faye turns out the lights and Lewis remains, for a moment, bent over the sleeping man. Amazing, that this person is Albert St. Dennis! *This* person. Though Lewis is going to argue against the worth of St. Dennis's poetry as part of his contention that all such art, such consciously wrought art, is no longer valid for our era, he has always acknowledged the fact that St. Dennis's poetry is poetry of surpassing beauty and power—a remarkable body of work. And this person, this sleeping grandfatherly person, is the poet himself.... Or was.

"Lewis?" Faye whispers. "Is something wrong? Shouldn't we—"

"Shut up," Lewis says.

He is blinking tears out of his eyes.

By 1:30 the Hochbergs are asleep in their three-bedroom colonial house out on the Old Armory Drive, Warren in his own room, Vivian in hers; Vivian lies awake for a while, thinking of that new, young girl—Sandra Jaeger—whom she had introduced to Lewis Seidel, and of Marilyn Byrne's comically desperate attempt to salvage the evening; and of the dinner party she will give in a few weeks, Albert St. Dennis the guest of honor, and the Garretts...if President Garrett is in town...and the Haases, whom Warren finds tolerable...and Gladys Fetler, whom everyone likes...and the Seidels, probably: despite Faye...and the Housleys...though maybe not the Housleys, since Mina has been so distracted lately...a look, almost, of the convalescent about her...a married daughter dying of cancer, it is said, in a clinic in Buffalo; so sad!...but Mina's presence is rather depressing as a result....Anyone else from the department? Not that foul-mouthed Brigit Stott, of course; and not the young people, not to so important a party; Gowan Vaughan-Jones, perhaps, though he says so little and hardly eats or drinks, merely looks from person to person, squinting and frowning, no doubt thinking of his work: one of the most brilliant men in his field, Warren believes, and only thirty-five years old....Possibly Gowan, then. And Lewis, has she counted him? Lewis and Faye. Cannot avoid. Year after year after year, Woodslee a small town, thrown together, cannot avoid, might as well accept. Make the best of. Rejoice, even.

She falls asleep, a handsome woman in her late forties, married now for...how many years?...can't recall: seventeen, nineteen, twenty. Or more. She falls asleep, thinking of a party. Thinking of the table, the candles, the water goblets, the wine glasses, the floral centerpiece, the china and the silverware and the linen napkins and...and....And....

By 2 A.M. nearly everyone is asleep except Brigit and Alexis, and Lewis, and Oliver Byrne, and Sandra Jaeger. Brigit and Alexis lie in Brigit's bed, in the rumpled, damp sheets, stroking each other sleepily, in the aftermath of love, dazed by the phenomenon of what has happened, rather drunk, unquestioning, not even uncomfortable yet; not even self-conscious and embarrassed yet. By 2:35 both are asleep. Oliver Byrne walks about the downstairs of his house, quietly, putting things away, rinsing plates and glasses, setting them in the automatic dishwasher. Marilyn is upstairs in bed; she nearly collapsed when the last of the guests left. Oliver, too restless to sleep, rather enjoys these oases of time after the excitement of a party, during which he can walk from room to room, unimpeded, partly undressed, in his bedroom slippers, putting his house in order. *His* house, *his* party. *His* guests. Brushing cigarette ashes from the piano—checking rather anxiously to see if—no?—no burns?—he tries to recall Alexis Kessler's piece. Difficult, tricky music; perhaps a parody—? Something meretricious about Kessler, unsettling. Ryerson saying of him he can't be trusted; can't take responsibility for his students falling in love with him; can't see how he invites infatuations, tragic misunderstandings. And that pouty swollen look of his....Oliver draws his fingers lightly across the piano keys. Undeniable talent in Kessler. How did the piece go? Reminiscent of Bartok. Or Ives. Erik Satie? Puzzling. Seductive. Not for Oliver to grasp. Long ago he learned *Clair de Lune* and *Sonate Pathétique* and the "Moonlight Sonata" and certain manageable pieces by Chopin and Liszt and Rachmaninoff and Ravel, but years have passed since he has even attempted them, since he has even allowed himself to think of attempting them, and of the humiliation he would certainly experience; his mind snapped one day when he was working on Ravel's *Jeux d'Eau*....(A piece he has heard Alexis Kessler play while semidrunk, with a certain flamboyant contempt.) Music was not his primary interest anyway; he earned his degrees in English history of the Elizabethan and Jacobean periods, published his dissertation at the age of twenty-eight, and was drawn into university politics the first year of his first appointment, at the University of Pennsylvania. An assistant dean at thirty-one, a dean at thirty-five, Dean of Humanities here at Woodslee at forty-two, and a most promising future, as everyone keeps telling him.... How did Kessler's piece go? Oliver would like to ask him for a copy of it, but he knows Kessler would only be amused and sarcastic, imagining that Oliver is patronizing him. The boy's suspicious nature.... Oliver knows Kessler is unreliable, but he intends to keep him at Woodslee just the same: Kessler became an issue last year when a number of his colleagues in the music department wanted him fired, and Oliver defended him, and does not intend to back down. He never backs down. Any sign of weakness would immediately be taken advantage of by his enemies.

He walks from room to room, carrying ashtrays, glasses, plates. He is not very efficient. How pleasant to be alone after that crush of people, how marvelous to relax, no conversations, no pose to be maintained, no anxiety over certain of his guests and their disappointing behavior, no constant checking of his wife, to see if—? To see if she is getting nervous. If her hands are trembling. He is cleaning up after a party, he is putting his house back in order. All is well. He will not think of Albert St. Dennis, of the man's ashen face, his broken voice, the tears that welled up in his eyes as he stammered his apology.... He will not think of Lewis Seidel's arrogance. Instead he relives the party as a series of tableaux, frozen in the mind's eye. So perfect is his recall, and so visual, that he can count his guests if he wishes. Count heads. (He has a habit of counting heads—at parties, at meetings of the university senate, even in stores or on the street.) His party, his guests. His lovely house. He counts them now, the people who came to his home tonight and helped to make his party a success: his supporters, his friends, his admirers. He is very fond of them. He wants only to be very fond of them. Someday Woodslee, New York, will be known as a center of the arts, a true community of artists, scholars, teachers, humanists...a community unique in this part of the world, perhaps in all the United States...a place where talented people from all parts of the world will meet. Not an impossible dream, is it? Not too ambitious.

He rinses glasses. Rubs lipstick stains off with his thumb. Empties ashtrays into the trash basket beneath the sink. So many smokers! Unfortunate habit. He throws crumpled napkins into an untidy heap. Ugh, the napkins used to wipe up St. Dennis's vomit....Might as well discard with the trash. Too disgusting to send to the laundry....Poor Marilyn, her hysteria in the kitchen after the last of the guests left. Good-by good-by good-by Gladys, good-by Roger and Charlotte, so happy you could come, so very happy, very very happy. Another vomit-stained napkin? Throw out with the rest.

By 2:00 he has cleaned as much as he can, taking his time, in no hurry. He can't, of course, plug in the vacuum cleaner or start the dishwasher. By 2:30 he is asleep, in the twin bed beside his wife's bed, suddenly exhausted, his spirit quite drained from him. The day had begun, hadn't it, with an 8:30 A.M. emergency meeting at the university, so many hours ago, a small lifetime ago, the Romance languages department in a state of chaos, the head of the department in a fierce struggle with some of his senior men, threats of violence, threats of actual murder, emergency meeting at 8:30 A.M. in secret, and what had he done afterward?...luncheon with the Dean of Men....The hours, the hours. Falling asleep he hears Alexis Kessler's music. He hears his friends' voices uplifted. They are happy together, they are laughing together, he has made this miracle possible. His guests, his miracle. Continuing miracle. In rapid succession his friends' faces appear and disappear: last of all he sees Lewis Seidel's jocose, maddening smile, one eyelid twitching, as it often does. And then a person whose face is unclear. A vapor. Shadows for eyes, a gaping hole for a mouth. Who...?

Stranger. Can't see. Lost.

He sleeps.

By 3 A.M. Lewis Seidel is asleep beside his wife, snoring fitfully. Because he perspires so much at night he is wearing not only his pajamas but a T-shirt and shorts. At about 5:30 he will probably awaken, soaking wet, shivering, and go to the bathroom, and change into a clean pair of shorts and another T-shirt; but now he is sleeping soundly. He stayed up for a while, downstairs, though Faye wanted him to come to bed. But no, he wasn't ready for sleep, his mind was too jumpy for sleep. He was thinking of....But he did not want to think about St. Dennis; he wanted to relax. He opened a can of ale and sat at the kitchen table, leafing through last Sunday's *New York Times Magazine*, which he had already read. Driving back from St. Dennis's he had turned deliberately down Linwood to see if Brigit's light was still burning...and it was, she was still up...and he wondered suddenly if he might drop Faye off at the house and make some excuse about checking St. Dennis again...wondered if he might circle back and ring Brigit's doorbell...invite himself up for a nightcap. They are friends, after all. Have much in common. A department of thirty people and among them only three or four you could talk to; must be lonely for Brigit. He considered dropping in, giving her the opportunity to apologize for having been rude; possibly telling her how annoyed he often was with her, though he supposed she couldn't help it, she was quick and witty and did not suffer fools gladly, which was why...which was why he had always liked her...which was why, in fact, he had hired her at Woodslee. Oh, didn't she know that?—that *he* had hired her? He might tell her he was quite fond of her; might ask her what she thought of him. The late hour...the alcohol... the good cheer of a party...the loneliness of her life... trauma of divorce...need for affection, for touching, for sex....

But he said nothing to Faye, he merely parked the car in the garage, suddenly too tired to drive out again.

Enough for one night. A successful evening, he had acquitted himself well, had caught the respectful ear of St. Dennis, had driven him home, had initiated what would probably be a long-lasting friendship...enough for one night. He drank ale, he leafed through the *Times*, he waited until he was really exhausted before going up to bed (lying awake has begun to terrify him for some reason: he is too keenly aware of his own heartbeat and of his wife's presence close beside him, her small moans and twitches and sighs). Then sleep. Sleep. So much to think of, must sleep...! St. Dennis and Brigit and Byrne and Alexis and Faye and Vivian and the others, the others, and his classes on Monday, two large sprawling adoring classes of undergraduates, lectures not yet organized, the thought of Sunday evening depressing, must telephone Brigit next week...must insist upon her understanding him....

The bitch.

By 3 A.M. only Sandra Jaeger is still awake. She is sitting in the imitation leather chair bought only two weeks ago at a discount store downtown, in her blue flannel bathrobe with the rosebuds embroidered on the collar and the satiny belt, her long narrow pale feet, bare, tucked beneath her. She is too excited to sleep. She is more excited now than she was at the party. An almost erotic sensation courses through her; she has experienced it before, after other parties, and finds it halfway pleasant.

She sits in the black leather chair, turning the pages of a journal. It has a dull red cover; it resembles a ledger book. A diary, a disconnected series of impressions, random entries in Sandra Baird's life, Sandra Baird Jaeger's life. Begun when she was eighteen, a freshman at Boston University six years ago.

Only six years—! Sometimes it frightens Sandra, to realize she has come so far.

She turns the pages, rereads her most recent entry—which has to do with the faculty wives' tea of last week, an event she had anticipated with excitement but that had disappointed her terribly, though it was not a total loss because she and Carol Swanson had gone together; she takes up a ballpoint pen, one of the many Ernest has left lying around the apartment, and begins to write about the Byrnes' party. Her make-up has been cleaned off carefully and she looks young and fierce and pure, and rather impatient. So much to record! So much to assimilate and comprehend!

The erotic excitement stays with her. It is not physical so much as mental. The desire to write down her impressions...to sort out, to analyze, to make clear....From time to time she gazes at the wall opposite at the inexpensive Cezanne print framed in a simulated walnut frame, from Woolworth's; from time to time she finds herself staring at the orange shag rug, without seeing it; she is in a kind of trance. Her eyes are opened wide and unseeing, an unclouded depthless blue. Her skin glows with defiant good health. She can hear her pulse in the silence; sleep will be impossible for many hours. Going to bed, slipping in beside Ernest: impossible.

She hopes he won't wake, as he sometimes does, and call out for her. And come looking for her.

She relives the party. She sees herself there, in the Byrnes' living room, at the center of that group of fascinating people. And how remarkable it was, as she and Ernest and the Swansons said repeatedly, their being invited to such an important function...a party in honor of Albert St. Dennis. (Ernest had found out, inadvertently, earlier that week, that the young man who shared his office—Bradley Keough—had *not* been invited.) It must have to do with the dean's interest in the younger faculty. They are so very fortunate to be here, at Woodslee, to have fled that dismal heartbreaking place in Trenton, New Jersey, that had almost destroyed Ernest; their good fortune makes Sandra tremble, it is so precarious, so amazing. And the Swansons are, if possible, even more grateful: Barry hadn't even had a job the year before, and Carol had worked fifty hours a week as a clerk-typist in Scranton. Now everything has changed. Their lives have changed. Their real lives have begun.

She sees again the handsome living room, the highly polished surfaces, the fresh-cut flowers, the lovely rug. The piano. The doors to the terrace open, a bright moon, everything marvelous, perfect. Mrs. Byrne speaking to her so warmly. Asking her and Carol about their impressions of Woodslee. About their apartment-hunting. Recommending stores in town, a grocery store out at the new mall.... Attractive woman. Early forties? Gracious, charming, kind. Expensively dressed. Allowed Sandra and Carol to help her with the food, passing things around. Dean Byrne so kind also. A little distracted at times, eyes darting about the room, handsome man in mid-forties, beginning to lose his hair, gray eyes, easy gracious smile. Remembered Ernest's name. Seemed impressed with Sandra—her master's degree in library science. (It has already been arranged, informally, that Sandra will have a part-time position at the library; when the budget is stabilized in another week or two, when the library determines how much part-time staff it will be allowed, Sandra will be working there. Ernest's previous college, that wretched extension in Trenton, had promised Sandra a job semester after semester but something had always gone wrong.) Was impressed, perhaps, with her looks also. Staring at her, smiling, smiling. Gray eyes. Dark gray. And hers blue, that startling pale blue....

She knows she is pretty, how could she not know? She has been told for so many years. By so many people. Pretty blue-eyed Sandra Baird.... She must take good care of her skin and her hair, must be aware of her posture, her clothes. (Tonight the lavender dress with the long dipping skirt: perfect.) She is pretty and she is intelligent, how could she not be aware of her good fortune...? The dean staring at her and smiling, asking about her background, Ernest's background, their impressions of Woodslee—the architecture is so striking, isn't it, Brandford Chapel most of all? Historic landmark. Built 1851. Dean Byrne shaking hands with his guests, introducing them to Sandra and Ernest as if they were equals, all of them equals. The odor of furniture polish, of cut flowers, of perfume. She is dizzy even now, remembering.

That sound? Her pulse. Heartbeat.

Impossible to sleep tonight!

She has been an insomniac since the age of fourteen. At first it alarmed her, and worried her parents, but now she hardly cares—now she is rather proud of it. Ernest worries; Ernest loves her very much. In a way, though, he is proud of her too—her sensitivity, her imagination. (What a contrast with Carol Swanson who, when the four of them met for dinner at a cheap Italian restaurant near the university, said something crudely sentimental about a man in a wheelchair, wheeled up to a nearby table—Sandra cannot remember the exact words, but they were mawkish and embarrassing, even Barry was embarrassed, and Sandra and Ernest exchanged a look of sheer surprise.) He has boasted within her hearing that his delicate little wife can get along on three or four hours' sleep a night.

The excitement is with her still; she writes as quickly as she can, covering page after page in the journal. Her handwriting is large and clear, girlish in its loops and dotted *i*'s. Ernest admires it: his own handwriting is small and severely slanted, almost unreadable. Everything you do is so lovely, he says; so beautiful. (They have been married a little over two years.)

In his eyes, that look of love.

In others' eyes, admiration...sudden interest... assessment. At times, it must be admitted, jealousy. (One of the women at the party tonight, middle-aged, rather plump, powdered: whose wife? Looking at Sandra with a queer listless expression. Not very friendly.) But she is accustomed to jealousy and envy, even to spite. In high school certain friends of hers talked behind her back, tried to hurt her feelings, tried to come between Sandra and her boy friends, and all because they were jealous of her good looks and her popularity. Now that she is married things are different—young women don't feel she is competing with them so directly—but there is still a sense of rivalry; in a way it exhilarates her. What Ernest said when they came home was true: *She was the most beautiful woman at the party tonight.*

Again she sees herself in the lavender dress, her hair swinging about her face, the thin silver chain about her throat. Mrs. Jaeger. Ernest Jaeger's wife. A clear, cool, melodic voice; long graceful legs; fashionable open-backed shoes. (The most expensive pair of shoes she has ever bought—$29.98.) She sees, again, Albert St. Dennis as he is being introduced to her: surprising, he is so much shorter than she had imagined. An old, old man. Face wrinkled but beautiful in its way. Must be eighty, eighty-five years old? So famous. No longer quite real. Evidently a little deaf. (Impossible to believe she will ever be that old—her skin lined and creased like that—really impossible. She cannot even imagine herself Mrs. Byrne's age.) Albert St. Dennis shaking hands with her, mumbling something she couldn't quite make out. He seemed very sweet, though; wasn't rude to her at all.... And Dr. Hochberg, head of Ernest's department, with his metal-rimmed glasses and his peculiar downward smile, his nasal voice—a little awkward with her but friendly enough, asking if she and Ernest were settled in their duplex apartment yet; something chilling about him, but Sandra is prepared to discover he is really very sweet. (Like a shy, reserved sociology professor she had had as an undergraduate.) He is certainly a brilliant man; Ernest said of his book on Dryden that it is a masterpiece of scholarship.... Most surprising of all was Mrs. Hochberg's interest in Sandra. Innumerable questions about plans for children, Sandra's hometown, Sandra's opinion of Boston. A woman in her fifties, perhaps, with graying hair, stern good looks, a slightly sardonic manner. Mole on upper lip: wonder why she doesn't have it removed. Must have been quite attractive at one time. Evidently charmed with Sandra, not at all jealous, taking her around to meet other guests. So many people...! Dr. Fetler, tall and white-haired and grandmotherly; Dr. Seidel, moon-faced, scowling and grinning, shrewd, rather forward— saying playfully, with a wink at Mrs. Hochberg, that it was too bad Sandra was married; Dr. Vaughan-Jones, with his loose, strengthless handshake and his gray-green teeth and his slight stammer—a young-old man whom Ernest admires very much also. And Brigit Stott, the novelist. Strange angular-faced woman, high cheekbones, messy hair, black dress falling below her knees, something melancholy about her—and that low husky almost inaudible voice—glittery-eyed as if on drugs—but friendly enough in her queer, chilled way; she actually smiled at Sandra, though she had nothing to say to her. Must have been a friend of St. Dennis's: took care of him when he was sick. A friend, too, of that bizarre young man with the bleached hair—the pianist—who had not once glanced at Sandra or Ernest or the Swansons. ("A homosexual," Carol said afterward, "wasn't he—?") Sweetest of all the guests was Mrs. Housley, the wife of the Chaucer specialist, a woman in her early sixties who must have weighed 160 or 170 pounds and who stood no higher than Sandra's chin—they had had a conversation during dinner about the town of Woodslee, about its handsome old Victorian homes that were in danger of being razed, its mills and factories that caused such problems, downriver especially, its loss of population, the poverty of its French-speaking section, the poverty in general, financial crises year after year after year, as long as Mrs. Housley could remember.... The woman was passionate and quite articulate. Worst of all, she said, was the fact that the town of Woodslee was invisible from the university's point of view. It was really arrogant of the university people, wasn't it, to refuse to take seriously the locality in which they lived and worked—? Sandra agreed. She listened closely, she was very polite. Mrs. Housley must have liked her because she mentioned something about Sandra coming over for tea sometime soon.... Afterward, when the party was over and Sandra and Ernest and the Swansons were getting into the Swansons' car, parked a few houses up from the Byrnes', the Housleys were standing by their car, talking loudly, and Sandra thought perhaps she should ask if something was wrong—and it turned out (according to Mrs. Housley, who seemed quite upset) that someone had broken into the Housleys' car during the party; one of the rear windows had been broken, the door unlocked, and a few items of no great value stolen—an umbrella, Mrs. Housley said, and an old valise.

Fortunately the Swansons' car had not been broken into; there were only a few books in the back seat.

"We just don't have crime in Woodslee," Mrs. Housley said, astonished.

Sandra, writing, pauses to look up: does she hear something?

Someone?

No. Silence.

Only a car with a faulty muffler out on Van Buren. What time—?

Almost 3:30

She is not yet ready for bed; she is still alert, excited, exhilarated. If only she could explain her queer, passionate yearning to Ernest—her sense of things being almost too wonderful, too enormous, for her to grasp. She knows she is very lucky, for instance. Her marriage to Ernest Jaeger was a stroke of good fortune. Their coming here to Woodslee, Ernest's appointment as an assistant professor—it is almost too wonderful, it is almost unreal. Many of Ernest's former classmates from Harvard have not yet found positions, even in junior or community colleges, or in high schools, and no one of their acquaintance has a job as good as Ernest's. Of course Ernest is an outstanding young man. He worked for several years on his Ph.D. dissertation, which was nearly seven hundred pages upon completion, and which is to be published by the University of North Carolina Press; his professors think very highly of him; everyone thinks highly of him. He is an experienced teacher—twenty-nine years old—by no means a beginner. He is industrious, dedicated, brilliant. ...Still, there are former classmates of his who have worked almost as hard, and who are almost as dedicated and as brilliant. Sandra thinks of them with pity. Some are bachelors, which makes their unemployment easier in one sense but more difficult in another, since they live alone; others are married, some even have children. When Ernest was offered that position of instructor at a university extension in Trenton everyone was envious, even a little bitter. He had not yet finished his Ph.D.; he had not seemed, on paper, so qualified as some of his friends.

In fact Ernest had lost a close friend at that time, a young man who had sent out two hundred fifty letters of application, without results, and who had come to think that his letters of recommendation were betrayals, that former professors were plotting against him, conspiring to ruin his career. His thinking was so twisted that he had convinced himself that his classmates—Ernest among them—stole his mail from his university mailbox and talked behind his back to professors. His grin became fixed, demonic. Another classmate of Ernest's, a brilliant young woman with an M.A. degree from Johns Hopkins whom Sandra had known fairly well and had liked, was still jobless after two years of applying to innumerable universities and colleges... and Sandra had heard, only the other day, of a suicide attempt, and hospitalization. Should she write to the girl? Dare she write? (For the fact of Ernest's excellent position could not have failed to depress her.) And there are other, wilder tales. Too improbable, in a sense, not to be true. A married couple with advanced degrees—hers in English, his in political science—were reported to have been seen in a massage parlor off Times Square (but who would have seen them, who would have confessed to having seen them in such a place?) where they were both employed. An attractive older student, a woman in her mid-thirties, was said to have abandoned her doctoral dissertation and to have agreed to marry into a harem—in Turkey, was it?—somewhere distant and exotic; she had met a very attractive, wealthy Middle Eastern man on a recent trip to England, and had been, so rumor had it, "quite easily seduced." There was a former friend of a friend said to be in jail, having been arrested for selling heroin to high-school students; or was it marijuana, merely; or had he been caught up in a police raid on a commune in Boston, and unfairly charged with possession of drugs, and unfairly treated.... There were outlandish and equally distressing tales of petty thievery, prostitution, gambling, and madness.

Sandra wonders: Should I feel grief for them. Should I care.

There are too many of us now.

Better not to think about the situation. Better to put it all behind her. After all, their lives have changed completely now. They are no longer graduate students: they are adults, with a genuine place in an academic community. Ernest is not a teaching assistant, he is an assistant professor of English, on what is called the regular payroll; and Sandra is on a list, a marvelous list, of names that belong to faculty wives. Some years ago, in the late sixties and early seventies, it might have seemed inconceivable that anyone, particularly bright young intellectuals, would have prized such things so highly, and so desperately; but it is no longer the late sixties and the early seventies.

Our friends wouldn't have cared about us, if Ernest and I had failed, Sandra thinks. There isn't time any longer to care.

A little sleepier now, she begins to think of a party. She and Ernest will give a party. In a few months, perhaps. A small party, because the living room here is so small. . . . A dinner party. She could prepare something special, something elaborate; beef Wellington, perhaps; she believes she might be an excellent cook if she tried. And Ernest could help her. And the other women would be quite impressed. And they would go away saying nice things about her. And their husbands, their husbands too, they would go away saying nice things about her, and about Ernest, and. . . .

A small dinner party for those people who have been especially friendly.

But—would it be premature? Would it appear to be presumptuous?

Possibly.

There was gossip, year before last, of an assistant professor's wife who had been too eager, too aggressive, who had made the error of inviting senior faculty members and their wives to her home far too quickly, and what had happened to her and her husband. . . what had been their fate...? Even the graduate students had known, and had laughed.

Sandra will wait; she will be cautious, and observant, and she will wait.

At the Seidels'

November 5, 8 p.m.

There he sits, on stage, diminutive, child-sized, so aged—by the glare of the lighting—as to seem no longer human, but a figure out of mythology.

In a navy blue three-piece suit bought for this occasion, in a starched white shirt with a stiff collar, a dark tie knotted tightly and perfectly at his throat and tucked down inside his vest, Albert St. Dennis sits, rigid and short-legged, very pale, staring out into the crowded twilight of the unfamiliar auditorium. His skin is luminous; his scalp gleams whitely through his thin fluffy hair; his glasses catch and reflect light in random sliver-like blinks. He stares at the crowd, the crowd stares at him. One abyss into another. What does he resemble, sitting there so properly?—a doll? His skin is pale, oyster-pale; it looks powdered. His mouth seems to have disappeared. His hands—which seem very small—are resting on his lap, motionless, atop a manila envelope. Feet also small: shoes that look new and are smartly polished. He is dressed properly and sedately, like an Englishman or a businessman or a small-town lawyer. His stomach churns with mild regret—he had only a small portion of his dinner, but perhaps even that was an error.

(Since 5:30 he has been herded about by busy friendly fussing bullying people, helped into and out of automobiles, an umbrella held ineffectually over his head to protect him against the sudden cold rain; he has been served cocktails, hors d'oeuvres, various courses of a lengthy and confused dinner at the president's house in the company of innumerable people, most of them strangers—President Garrett himself was unfortunately absent from the dinner, having flown to San Francisco to attend a national conference of university presidents only that morning.)

He is staring patiently at his audience, at the rows and rows of faces. So many people...! Even the air is jostled and overheated. All the seats in Brandford Hall appear to be filled. Were filled, Dean Byrne informed him, half an hour ago. Students, professors, wives, people from town and perhaps even from nearby cities: row upon row extending out of sight. More are standing at the rear and in the aisles. Some are sitting in the aisles. Who are these people, St. Dennis wonders, quietly alarmed; what do they expect from him...? So many, many strangers, all of them eager and watchful and curiously reverential. He wonders what perverse logic has assembled these people here tonight and brought him to sit before them, elevated above them like a minor, rather embarrassed god.

He blinks rapidly, scanning the first several rows. Familiar faces? Where?...His wife? No. He can't see beyond the first four rows.

8:00. 8:05. Still the hall is filling; doors at the rear are continually opening. A young man with shoulder-length hair approaches the stage and, twisting his body oddly, takes a photograph of St. Dennis. The flash of light is blinding.

His hands clasp each other firmly. Moist and cool. A secret handshake. He is frightened but he will manage to get through the reading as he has managed to get through many readings, and afterward people will congratulate him and there will be a party or a reception and then he and Harriet will leave together quietly and that will be that. A midnight reward: brandy, a few mints, and bed.

How many hours until then...? Only four.

But Harriet isn't with him, is she; no longer with him. He has crossed the wide storm-gray Atlantic alone. He is alone. "Poetry and the 'Eternal Affirmation of the Human Spirit.'" Alone on this enormous continent with only a frail skein of words to hold his life together.

The microphone is being adjusted; there are agressive coughing noises. Static that rises and becomes a high-pitched whine, and is then miraculously cut off. The audience quiets. Oliver Bryne is at the podium, shuffling through a half-dozen note cards. Dressed casually but impeccably in a sports jacket that is probably genuine camel's hair, a wide handsome striped necktie, shirt cuffs that are very white. St. Dennis has never seen Dean Byrne with glasses before; he looks fastidious and aristocratic, peering at the notecards as if he were entirely alone, absolutely at ease.

8:08. The evening begins.

A voice, many times amplified, fills the auditorium. It is grave and graceful and beautifully modulated. Its subject is Albert St. Dennis. "The most distinguished of living English poets." "A superb artist and craftsman, second only to Yeats himself in this century." How proud the voice is of its subject, how quietly triumphant it rings out...! St. Dennis stares at his clasped hands and wills that his spirit not slip out of his body; not tonight. It is unreal, all of it is unreal, lacking even that jarring hellish reality of a nightmare, which, however unpleasant, is nevertheless one's own. The voice that trumpets his excellence, the crowded hall, the blinding lights, the rows of indistinct faces, the endless cocktail hour, the endless dinner, those well-intentioned people querying him about his "impressions" of the United States and his "opinions" of the federal government—about which he knows nothing—and filling his wine glass with wine despite his prudent entreaties: unreal, all unreal. Yet it must be confronted. It must be acknowledged.

Thirty-seven books since 1926, when his first volume of poems, *Harlequin,* was published privately in London; books that have been translated into countless languages. Awards and prizes and medals and grants and commissions. Honorary degrees from English and European universities. Said to have been (and to be) considered for a Nobel Prize. Most famous for his poetry but also the author of distinguished prose works: a novel, several collections of essays, a travel book, the first volume of his autobiography. A libretto in 1955 in collaboration with Ralph Vaughan Williams. A verse play produced in London to critical acclaim and modest commercial success. Translations and editing of Russian and Greek and Czech poetry; a much-praised translation of *The Divine Comedy*, a brief but excellent critical biography of Hopkins, written in 1931. And on and on. St. Dennis has lived a long full life, a most formidable life; it sounds enviable. It sounds unbelievable.

He is staring at his hands, now fussing with the manila envelope. A sheaf of poems, written in longhand, in pencil. Rather messy. Difficult to read. New poems—fairly new—written within the past year. The poems are real enough. The smudged pages are real. Each of the words is his own. A skein of words, a strategy not of survival but of the costs of maintaining survival. Who will understand? Who in this crowded hall will understand? Words, frail and mortal. Sacred. "Albert St. Dennis" no longer recognizable except as a voice, a mouth, a spirit composed of words....

Oliver Byrne has shifted now, has backtracked to speak of St. Dennis's family history. His people were glassmakers in York in the eighteenth century; some of the family moved to London, gave up glassmaking and became merchants, small tradesmen, grocers. There was even a barrister or two in St. Dennis's branch of the family. St. Dennis himself was born in 1906 in Ealing. In public school and at New College, Oxford, he specialized in the classics. Married to Harriet Arnold, 1936. Co-editor of the avant-garde magazine *Proteus*, 1934–1939. Schoolteacher, clerk for an insurance firm in London, a year of medical school, British army (infantry), wounded in 1943. Travels to Greece, Egypt, Jerusalem, Persia, Russia, Australia. Controversial "Letters from Rhodesia" published in *New Statesman*, 1951–52. Many invitations over the years from the United States—many proffered awards—including a medal from the National Institute of Arts and Letters—but, until this year, St. Dennis had always declined to visit with his American admirers. Woodslee University is therefore very conscious of its good fortune, very honored to have been singled out by Albert St. Dennis for his first visit. The author of a number of modern classics, notably *The Explorers* and *Hecate,* the author of the tantalizing statement, "All art is absurdity," here with us tonight—here to give the first of his Woodslee readings—"Poetry and the 'Eternal Affirmation of the Human Spirit'"—

The voice concludes; the audience applauds.

Elderly, hard of hearing, short of leg and of breath, dim-visioned, uncomfortably warm, slightly sick to his stomach; peering with elfin solicitude into the cavernous hall, who is this person who has accomplished this lifetime...? The strangers are applauding enthusiastically. Applause brings St. Dennis to his feet. He knows he is an imposter, he knows he is taking advantage of his American hosts' gullibility, but they are applauding as if eager for his poetry, his wisdom— "All art is absurdity," what can that possibly mean?—what could it have ever meant?—as if eager for his being itself. And so he rises as Dean Byrne turns to him, smiling, as the applause flows in waves about him. He does not know who he is, who they expect him to be, he has forgotten most of his life and does not care to summon it back, but the Dean's generous introduction and the audience's generous applause awaken him to his duty: he is to impersonate "Albert St. Dennis" for the next hour.

He begins with a line from Keats: "The poetry of earth is never dead."

At first his voice quavers. Then, gradually, it regains its fragile strength. He hears himself speaking as if from a distance. Earth, poetry, craftsmanship, labor, love, despair, joy, the necessary restrictions of art. He is shuffling unobtrusively through his papers. He selects a poem—some relationship to the line of Keats?—he can't quite remember the connection though he is certain there is one—ah yes: poetry of earth never dead. Deathlessness of the human spirit, that point at which art and nature converge. Communion of mankind through language. Yes.

He reads his first poem, a soliloquy set in a garden.

An autumn garden, it is. Friends' home in Rottingdean. Allusions to Hardy's garden poems—will his audience understand? Hardy a mourner and a survivor like St. Dennis, a widower like St. Dennis. The kinship of loss. Brotherhood. Someone has died—someone has always died. One by one by one: mother, father, grandparents, cousins, friends, many friends, enemies as well. Sunlight becoming ever more powerful, glaring, merciless, no shadows remaining in the old, untidy garden, everything exposed and broken. Someone has died. Wife? Forty years married. Forty years. (The hushed amazement of the young; perhaps a little embarrassed.) A poem worked and reworked innumerable times. Torture, the refinement of emotion into art. As Auden spoke of an estrangement between oneself and one's name, so there is an estrangement between oneself laboring in the present and oneself laboring in the past; yesterday's triumphs are today's embarrassments. What was tragic becomes merely anecdotal. Is grief that can be so ingeniously measured grief any longer...? But the cunning of the poet knows no limit.... He is reading the poem slowly and again his voice quavers. (To his shame he broke down once during a reading, in London; long before his wife's death, however. Could never understand, afterward, why his own poetry, at that particular moment, had seemed to him too painful to be borne. But it had torn into him, had torn from him a sobbing cry.)...The autumn sunlight, a glaring golden haze; the parched earth; the hazards of love and survival. An old man scribbling in a ledger book. Secretive. Secretive as a boy of six, secretive as an old man of seventy. Character is fate, unchanging. Nothing changes. Scribbling the inexpressible until his cold blood heats. Whirlwind. Swirlwind. Endless teasing of sounds. Anonymity of art when one surrenders entirely to it, delicious privacy of perfection, inexpressible joy. He does not dare hope that anyone else can understand.

The garden soliloquy came to him as if dictated from without, from a source beyond him. Something to do with Harriet, perhaps—her poor pain-wracked spirit? Bodiless. Teasing. A poem of more than one hundred lines in its first version, a terrible pressure of words, flood of words, crowding one another in his small slanted handwriting until his fingers ached. Arthritic anyway, knuckles slightly swollen. A poem that forced itself out onto the page, gave birth to itself, as certain other poems of his had, over the years, flowing through him, animating him, using him. For some time before the writing he had felt extremely cold, chilled, yet in a state of impersonal euphoria. Time had stopped. There was no time. How, then, to burst into his own life, claim his own being again, give a legendary quality to his own commonplace grief...?

An hour's feverish scribbling and then exhaustion. Upstairs to nap, a nervous fretful evening, no appetite for dinner, alone in his room with the challenge of the poem, the mad torrent of words, working and reworking it through the night. As if he were still a young man. As if his life were still before him. Monologue. Grief. Finding the right words, the perfect rhythm.... Trying to recall a poem already written, complete.... A voice not his. Superior to his. Vocabulary deliberately austere, pared back, ruthlessly denuded of the gorgeous, the dramatic, the "poetic." *Memento mori*. Untranslatable emotion. His masters Dante and Shakespeare and Yeats cannot help him here. Experience of having lived—of having lived as himself—yearning now for anonymity, for peace—

He has finished reading the poem. Suddenly it is over. He glances up, startled, timid, like an uncertain lover.

The applause begins immediately, then dies back: as if the audience, though deeply moved, fears intruding upon his grief. But then he blinks and manages a confused smile, and they take heart and applaud again, rather more loudly than he recalls other audiences having applauded in the past, back home. He stares out at the rows and rows of strangers. They *are* deeply moved. The poem does mean something to them. And they are grateful for their own emotion—grateful to be allowed to show that they possess emotion—

He blinks tears from his eyes, embarrassed, flattered, shuffling through his messy papers. For some reason he had not expected things to go so well, he had not expected such warmth, such enthusiasm, perhaps it was not a mistake to come to North America, perhaps this will be a turning point in his life....

He is, after all, "Albert St. Dennis."

Oh God, Brigit thinks, *I love you.*

It is Alexis she loves, it is St. Dennis she loves. The young man sitting beside her, scented, his thigh pressed against hers, his arms folded; the old man behind the lectern, peering out at his audience as if perplexed by their response. The rumors were false: St. Dennis is in excellent health and he isn't drunk and his voice is frail but authoritative and he reads his poems beautifully and the entire hall is under a kind of enchantment....

"Thank God he's all right," Brigit whispers to Alexis. Her eyes have filled with tears and she hopes they won't spill and run down her cheeks; what if someone notices...! People have been looking rather curiously at her this evening.

"Yes," Alexis says. "You shouldn't have worried."

They are sitting near the back of the auditorium, having come just before eight o'clock when most of the seats were already taken. It is the first time the two of them have appeared in public, in Woodslee, except for a few walks along the river and dinner one evening in a downtown hotel; their sitting side by side tonight has the look, Brigit believes, of an accident. No one can see how they are pressed together in the dark, thigh to thigh, knee to knee, or how Alexis has reached beneath his own arm to grasp her fingers in his, in secret, so that they are holding hands like children, undetected. Both are quite well dressed: Alexis is wearing a pale gold jacket of soft, fine wool, and a black turtleneck sweater, and Brigit is wearing a cashmere suit with a dark fur collar, and silver earrings that swing

106

heavily against her thin cheeks; if people glance at her it is probably because they have never seen her wearing earrings before. Nor have they seen her so striking, so well groomed. *Is* that Brigit Stott...?

With Alexis Kessler?

But it must be an accident.

For the past several days there were rumors that the reading would be postponed: St. Dennis had left Woodslee suddenly to fly back to London, having resigned his position; St. Dennis had had a breakdown of some sort; St. Dennis had had a heart attack, a stroke, a severe case of the intestinal flu now making the rounds of Woodslee, a quarrel with the administration, a failure of nerve. Brigit telephoned Oliver Byrne to see if there was any truth to the rumors and he denied them angrily, charging his "enemies" with slander. Over the weeks St. Dennis has made a varied impression on people. Some are struck by his warmth and kindness and his generosity with his time; others are hurt that he is aloof with them and interrupts their questions with rude questions of his own. One of Brigit's students, a young man named Todd Andress, who has committed much of St. Dennis's work to memory—he has a photographic memory, evidently—has visited St. Dennis in his office at the university and also in his apartment, and cannot stop praising him, rattling off St. Dennis's terse, gnomic remarks in a high excited voice; Andress is keeping a journal of his conversations with St. Dennis. Other students are uncomfortable with the old man because he so frequently murmurs Oh yes, yes, to their questions, nodding gravely, blinking at them through the slightly magnified lenses of his glasses. He is bored with them all, they say. No, but his mind is elsewhere—he is preoccupied with his own life, with his own work. Perhaps he is homesick for England...? Or is he merely deaf? Nodding courteously, he gives the impression of both hearing what people say and not hearing. And then there have been times when he's been quite impatient and has cut short an interview, saying he has an appointment elsewhere. Warren Hochberg has declared himself immensely pleased with St. Dennis. Rumors of the old man's drinking, his probable alcoholism?—totally unfounded. A rumor that he had telephoned the airport at Champlain the very next morning after the Byrnes' party in his honor to inquire about flights back to England—ridiculous. He is very happy at Woodslee. Very happy. (Vivian Hochberg telephoned Brigit one morning back in October to invite her to a dinner party that very evening because, as she said—Vivian Hochberg being, as everyone knows, a remarkable woman—Albert St. Dennis, who was the guest of honor, had specifically asked that Brigit be included in the party; Brigit and that young man with the amazing blond hair, the pianist, what was his name...? Brigit had declined the invitation, and Vivian had not troubled to plead with her or to disguise the subtle relief in her voice; Brigit and Vivian know each other as well as they care to, and there is no need for dissembling. But it was a surprising call and Brigit was quite moved by St. Dennis's interest in her.) Warren is officially pleased with his Distinguished Professor of Poetry, but Gowan Vaughan-Jones is rather hurt that St. Dennis hasn't much time for him—he had planned a series of taped interviews in conjunction with his study of twentieth-century poetics, and had even arranged with the editors of several prestigious journals for the publication of these interviews. But midway in the first session St. Dennis suddenly got to his feet and, coughing rather badly, cigarette in hand, told Gowan that he had nearly forgotten a luncheon date with an old friend—he was very sorry, but the interview would have to be postponed. (Gowan tells everyone the story, his expression mournful, his eyes moist as a dog's eyes, and receives their sympathy with a look of abject resignation; he is oblivious to the fact that, behind his back, his colleagues imitate his voice and repeat the story with extravagant variations and embellishments, and even Brigit, who finds Vaughan-Jones both pitiful and alarming (he is, after all, a widely published scholar, an expert in his field) cannot help but laugh at the Vaughan-Jones routines her colleagues do.)

Lewis Seidel has reported better luck, having taken St. Dennis to lunch at the Faculty Club a few times, and even down to the Riverview one Friday afternoon, where the old man was rather flattered by having been surrounded by young people, and where he had drunk innumerable glasses of beer as round after round was brought to the crowded table; but Lewis has complained that St. Dennis evades his questions and has fallen into the habit of talking without regard for his audience, of simply droning on and on...interesting monologues in themselves, sometimes fascinating, touching upon his mild friendship with the Huxleys, his boyhood interest in astronomy, his love of Agatha Christie and Dorothy Sayers mysteries, his old hobby of bird-watching, which he wished he might revive here in North America, if only his legs weren't so uncertain and his eyes so weak; his collection of biographies of Newton, which he regretted not having brought along to Woodslee; his love of jigsaw puzzles, of mushrooms and garlic and butter sauce, of toffee, of chocolate-coated biscuits, of Hollywood musicals of the forties; his hatred of travel by air and by car; his good-natured envy of American plumbing and heating and housing and salaries; his vehement hatred of the welfare state; his slightly slurred and perhaps, for that reason, not entirely serious expression of a wish that a "Stalin or a Hitler" might come along to "save" England; his love of Thomas Hardy's later poetry (which he recited at great length); his old quarrel with certain Krishnamurti disciples among his circle of friends; his old quarrel—a lover's quarrel, really—with the nominalists; his fascination with geology and the exploration of the earth and of space; his declaration that *The Explorers* was not only his own best work but the most important poem of the twentieth century, and that no one understood it, and that he intended to write a fifth section to extend the poem's metaphorical base so that it included space exploration—if only he were young enough, if only he were another person entirely, and might explore the "eternal silence of those infinite spaces" himself! Monologues sometimes delivered in a bright loose manner, a boy's smile raying across his face, but sometimes slow and dull and cold and slurred and really not very pleasant, so that his listeners shivered, wishing themselves elsewhere, while they nodded solemnly and made an effort to commit these strange words to memory.

It was said of St. Dennis that he began his day early, shortly after six, that he had fruit juice and coffee and a cigarette at his desk, that he worked steadily until noon—always writing: notes, drafts of essays, translations, reviews, prefaces, a journal, and of course poems, always poems, old drafts revised, new poems blocked out, even poems that were already published reworked and re-imagined; if he hadn't a luncheon engagement he made a simple meal for himself, usually soup (mushroom or vegetarian vegetable) and cheese (cheddar cheese of the mildest variety) and bread (rye or whole wheat), and then he returned to his work, to mail that must be answered, which he felt to be a necessity—an obligation. Always letters, most of them requesting favors of one kind or another, some enclosing poems for his comments: and he was courteous enough to reply to them all, or so it was said. Lewis Seidel remarked to him that his energies were being drained by these self-promoting strangers, these flatterers and con men; it would be wiser to hire a secretary to answer them and wisest of all merely to throw the letters away without reading them. St. Dennis had replied (or so it was said: Brigit got this story at many removes from the occasion) that, in *that* case, he would never have come to Woodslee University and would never have made Mr. Seidel's acquaintance.

He works an eight- to ten-hour day, either in his apartment or in his office at the university (where he spends most of Tuesday and Thursday afternoons); he is besieged by invitations for the evenings and is forced—with genuine regret, it seems—to decline most of them. A gentleman, hostesses say; a typical English snob, say those whose hospitality has been rejected. After Vivian telephoned Brigit it occurred to her that perhaps St. Dennis might really like to see her again...and so she wrote him a note, asking if she and her friend Alexis Kessler might take him to dinner one night; he had replied at once, warmly, but insisted that they come to *his* apartment; and so they had, arriving separately, elated and apprehensive and, as the curious

110

evening wore on, rather dismayed at St. Dennis's behavior—the dinner of smoked salmon and caviar and marinated mushrooms and rye bread with margarine was well-prepared, though oddly chosen, and the wine—a white German Rhine—was superb; but St. Dennis drank too much, in fact had drunk too much before Brigit and Alexis even arrived, his monologues were sleepy, near-inaudible, and it alarmed Brigit that he seemed to be addressing them as if he knew them very well, as if they were old, intimate friends who already knew most of what he was talking about or alluding to; as if, in short, they were someone other than Brigit Stott and Alexis Kessler. At the very end of the evening he had, however, wakened sufficiently to apologize for having bored them, and for the dinner, which he realized was somehow incomplete, lacking something—vegetables, of course!—there were carrots and fresh spinach and broccoli in one of the compartments of the refrigerator but he wasn't accustomed to the refrigerator and had overlooked them—would Brigit and Alexis please forgive him? And allow him to make up for the evening by coming to dinner again soon? Naturally they had protested that the dinner had been excellent, the evening's conversation excellent, there was no need for him to apologize, and it was they who wished to repay him, sometime soon, by taking him out to dinner or, if he preferred, by having him to dinner at Brigit's apartment, which was only a few blocks away....St. Dennis appeared to find this a delightful suggestion; he accepted at once. They suggested a day in two weeks' time, a Wednesday evening, and St. Dennis nodded enthusiastically, and when the evening came he simply didn't show up and neither Brigit nor Alexis dared telephone him. It crossed Brigit's mind that he hadn't really heard the details of the invitation and so could not be blamed for having failed to come.

They ate the dinner themselves and finished the wine and made love in Brigit's bed and, for several hours afterward, talked of old age, of their mutual fears of senility, and cancer, and the gradual atrophy of the body; they talked of their work and of St. Dennis's achievement; of friendships that had blossomed and died; of past loves; of how much they liked St. Dennis without knowing exactly why—was it because he was so famous, or because he was a genuinely lovable person?—was it possible, really, to distinguish between the two?—and did he suffer because of this confusion? In her lover's arms Brigit spoke of fears she would never dare admit to in other contexts; she told Alexis that it had become painfully obvious to her, during the evening at St. Dennis's, how little people can do for each other, ultimately—how little they can do most of all for someone that age, who has already lived his life, who is wrapped about in a cocoon of memories, hypnotized by his own voice. "People talk and other people appear to listen. People talk to relieve their loneliness and other people appear to listen to relieve their loneliness. Isn't that it? One by one they die of loneliness, they're suffocating of loneliness, but they don't know it....Or do you think they know it?"

Alexis murmured a sleepy reply, pressing against her. His breath was warm, his embrace warm, one of his legs was resting partway over one of hers, his penis stirred and hardened and ebbed again, pressed against her thigh; he murmured what sounded like *Yes* but Brigit could not be sure.

Now she sits beside him listening to St. Dennis's slow thin beautiful voice speak of love, of marriage, of death, of art. Her eyes are still stinging with tears. "All art is absurdity," St. Dennis has declared. There is a melancholy puckishness about the old man. Far from being shy before this impressive crowd, St. Dennis is addressing them as if he were speaking casually and frankly to a small gathering of acquaintances. Ah, a remarkable man! Perfectly in control. He is not the noble ruin Brigit had feared; he is clever, he is even a little theatrical, there is no mistaking his genius. Diminutive and appearing shy, he stands behind the lectern, reading poems of loss, of grief, of bitter despair; he is mortal in every syllable, utterly vulnerable, a widower confessing to his bewilderment at the cessation of his own despair; a man among men, questioning his own humanity. His poems are stark as exposed
112

bone. They are almost too painful to be shared. (They appear to be new poems—in manuscript—evidently written here in Woodslee.) The absurdity of poetry: its risks, its possibilities, its necessary defeats. Its explorations. Its occasional beauty. (Brigit's own work is temporarily stalled. It is balked, stopped, stuck; it may never move forward again. She wonders if it was not out of despair at her continuing failure to write her novel that she fell in love with Alexis Kessler, and fell in love with him so helplessly.)

Brigit, pressing against her lover as if for consolation, inhaling his scent, squeezing his fingers between her own, listens as St. Dennis tells them of the death of passion and the metamorphoses of the human spirit beyond even the point of despair, and the need of the poet, if he is to survive, to impoverish his own youthful language in the service of a simplicity as utterly ruthless and inevitable as death itself.

Poetry is an absurdity but a gorgeous absurdity: like civilization, like love, like the adventure of human life itself. A risk that must be taken. A risk that must be taken again and again, as long as we live.

My God, Brigit thinks, *I love you.* . . .

It is Alexis she loves.

Her spirit seems to have shifted from her, her center of gravity seems to lie outside her, now, yearning outward, desiring only to plunge into this man, this stranger.

She thinks of him constantly.

He is close as her pulse beat, close as the interior of her eyelid, the roof of her mouth. Away from him she experiences at times a sensation of actual vertigo at the thought of him, the memory of him—his voice, his eyes, his mouth, his hands, his body, his love-making—the incredible fact of him, that he should exist at all and that he should love her. It seems at such times that the two of them have known each other most of their lives, and that everyone must know of their love; when in fact no one in Woodslee knows or could guess. They have been discreet, secretive and cunning and jealous of their knowledge of each other.

Since that night in September Brigit has come to think of Alexis Kessler as the center of her life—not only her life at the present time, but her life in its entirety. The past has become insignificant. Her marriage—her feeling for Stanley—her feeling for one or two other men—have become meager and anemic and irrelevant to her truest self. In a sense the past is a delusion, an error. She has never known anyone like Alexis.

Nor is it likely that there is anyone like him, another man quite like him. He is the center of her imagination no less powerfully than if she had created him herself. Beyond the small, tight, intense universe of their passion the rest of the world is transparent, not altogether real. Once or twice he has asked her about Stanley, about her marriage; is it true she isn't yet divorced...? And she tells him hurriedly that the marriage doesn't matter, belongs to the past, she can't believe in it or remember her husband, not now, not any longer, not when she is with him.

"But you're married even now, even this minute...." Alexis says slowly, as if bemused.

"No. Not really," Brigit whispers.

For years no one had approached her. She had allowed no one near. There were men, there were even friends of Stanley's, and even a few men here at Woodslee, but she kept herself from them, fastidious and virginal and rather hateful—she had felt a certain revulsion at the mere thought of men, of love, of being touched again. What had passed between Stanley and her had been a kind of love, after all, and she wanted no more of it.

("Why don't you die," Stanley had whispered once, lying beside her, the two of them exhausted and tranquil in the mid-summer heat. "You're suicidal. You know you've always been suicidal. I promise not to lift a finger to stop you.")

She never thinks of her husband now. She thinks only of Alexis.

The edginess of early girlhood has returned and she finds herself anxious about mirrors—dreads glancing into them and yet cannot resist, needing to know how she appears to her lover. It no longer matters very much what she knows herself to be from the inside; her spirit has indeed shifted outside her body.

"I love you," one of them says.

"I love you," says the other.

No one had approached her for years. Yet Brigit and Alexis had risen as if their names had been called and, without knowing how it happened, they moved into each other's arms. She embraced him hungrily, he embraced her, they found themselves laughing with the surprise and the ease of it. Becoming lovers had been less difficult than having a conversation.... Alexis said to her afterward, "I would have been afraid to touch you," and she had said, "I would have been afraid to touch *you*," as if they had not, in fact, had to touch each other at all; as if neither had had to make the first move. Upstairs in Brigit's apartment, after Lewis Seidel had dropped them off, they had had several drinks and talked for a while about their lives here at Woodslee, their mutual dissatisfaction, their vague teasing hopes—they had not talked for very long, Brigit realized afterward—and then for some reason they had smiled strangely and rose and simply stepped into each other's arms.

And so it had begun.

The following weekend they left Woodslee after Brigit's class on Friday afternoon and drove to Montreal, where they stayed at the Sherbrooke Arms, not far from Mt. Royal. They walked for hours along the windy streets with their arms around each other, reckless and exhilarated. They were one hundred miles away from Woodslee, in a city of strangers. They were in a foreign country and in a very foreign city: the French spoken in Montreal did not resemble the French Brigit had learned in college and had spoken, with some awkward, minimal success, in France. Alexis, here in Montreal, speaking French rapidly and gracefully with waiters and shopkeepers and hotel personnel, seemed to Brigit a different person—less self-conscious than he was at Woodslee, less flamboyant and pretentious. There were many men on the streets near the hotel and on Rue de

La Montagne, some not so young, and none so attractive as Alexis, who dressed as colorfully as he, and his raw, abrasive, delighted laughter did not seem so startling. She no longer flinched when he burst into laughter as he often did; she found herself joining him. She too had a robust, hearty laugh, a way of laughing with her entire body, that she had not experienced for some time.

She had forgotten how much she liked to walk. How much she liked to walk in cities. It did not matter where, it did not matter what she found to look at, or into—the mere fact of walking was a delight in itself, a joy. At Woodslee she had sometimes walked along the river or in the arboretum west of the university, but she had never cared to walk in the residential sections, however attractive they were, because she was likely to meet someone who knew her, who would invariably feel the need to involve her in a strained, pointless conversation about the university or the weather or the scandal of local politics; and she had not liked to walk in the downtown area, which was becoming rather shabby. The only thing she really missed about New York City, apart from two or three friends, was her habit of taking long aimless solitary walks to clear her mind, during which she had plotted her way to a new life, erasing her errors and beginning again, unhusbanded, virginal, innocent. These long hours of walking had cultivated her interior voice until it seemed to her, at times, that she lived only in that voice, in that constant harangue, and would be extinguished if it were ever silenced.

Alexis also took great pleasure in walking, and he expressed surprise that Brigit—who was so slightly built—should be able to walk for hours without tiring. (It had seemed to Brigit that Alexis would tire quickly: she had seen him yawn so often at parties.) He was fascinated by people, as Brigit was, drawing near them to overhear their conversations, taking note of the qualities of their voices. He did not pay attention to what they said, as Brigit did; he cared for their intonations, for the music of their words. At times he was rather blatant about eavesdropping and did not seem to notice that others were aware of him. He carried himself with a peculiar aggressive innocence that Brigit had never seen in anyone else; it was one of the qualities in him that had seemed to her so annoying in the past, and now seemed so powerfully enchanting.

Like a child, he was insatiably curious. He found nothing dull in a street of ordinary stores; he enjoyed window-shopping without regard for the sort of merchandise he was looking at. He liked the pretentious boutiques in the ghastly underground palaces that tunneled beneath the city, honeycombed with innumerable stores and restaurants and cinemas. He loved to browse in bookstores, as Brigit did, and in record stores, and he loved to shop—he bought a two-volume set of Mozart's letters for Brigit, and a recording of Elliott Carter's *Variations for Orchestra,* he insisted upon buying Brigit the suit with the muskrat fur collar and bought himself a winter overcoat with a near-identical collar; he bought hand-tooled leather boots for himself on Rue de la Montagne, and tried to talk Brigit into buying an immense purse for herself in the same store; he bought her the earrings at a silversmith's in a basement shop near McGill University and another ring for himself; he encouraged her to buy a new pair of shoes with unusually high, chunky soles—he did not like the more conventional shoes Brigit customarily wore—and to buy a forty-five-dollar blouse of silky biege, though Brigit protested it was impractical and not her style at all. He insisted she make an appointment at the beauty salon in their hotel to have her hair cut and styled—couldn't she see how unbecoming her hair was, grown out so unevenly about her delicate face? Didn't she care that she was not nearly so attractive as she might be? He suggested, too, that she have her hair tinted. Silver streaks in dark hair were attractive, but not gray; there was no need, he said, for her to look years older than she was. She accepted his gifts with some reluctance; she bought the blouse but not the shoes, and not the purse; she agreed to have her hair styled but not tinted. She insisted upon paying for half the hotel bill, which was considerable. In the end, back at Woodslee, he had to borrow fifty dollars from her for grocery money, to last until October 1.

They spent a lazy Sunday in the hotel room, in bed most of the morning, drinking tea and eating croissants, reading through newspapers. It was extraordinary, how little the newspapers meant to them.... Politicians whose names Brigit had never heard of, photographed in attitudes of self-righteous anger; the president of the postal union calling for a general walkout; Quebecers' demands in regard to something called the "bilingual" bill; a speech made by a Progressive Conservative candidate for Parliament; a scandal involving a provincial health minister; the charges made by an NDP candidate that mercury poisoning among Quebec Indians was not being taken very seriously by Ottawa. It was disturbing in one way and reassuring in another, that the headlines and the articles and the photographs related to so little that Brigit and Alexis knew. "We should move to Canada," Alexis said gaily. "Nothing means anything here—we could be alone, we could be ourselves. There would be nothing significant to think about here. It's like passing through the looking glass and coming into another world. Or like waking up in Lilliput."

There were several articles on the crisis in unemployment and inflation, which Brigit scanned but could not take seriously; apart from New York City, Montreal seemed to her the most demonstrably and ostentatiously rich city she had ever visited. The high-rise apartment buildings, the hotels, the expensive restaurants and boutiques and nightclubs, the numerous people like themselves, tourists like themselves, strolling aimlessly and happily along the hilly streets and into the center city.... Even Canadian money—two-dollar bills, saffron-colored bills, fifty-dollar bills illustrated like comic strips—seemed unreal, like Monopoly money.

"It's hard to take seriously," Brigit agreed. "But I suppose we must."

"Why?" Alexis asked.

They lay together atop the enormous untidy bed and talked. Brigit and Alexis. Registered under the name Kessler for the sake of convenience only; in an excellent room on the fifteenth floor of the hotel, with a lovely view of the lower city. They kissed, they stroked each other, they yawned and talked and lit cigarettes, and stretched lazily, and smiled, and found themselves inordinately happy. Alexis spoke of his plans for the song cycle based on St. Dennis's poems; he had completed one of the songs so far and was fairly satisfied with it, though he hesitated to show it to anyone. He spoke of his uncertain position at Woodslee. It baffled him that any of his colleagues should hate him enough to send him anonymous letters or make anonymous late-night telephone calls, as they sometimes did, or spread amazing rumors about him; worst of all was the knowledge that people wanted him fired—didn't they know how much he depended upon his job, not only financially but emotionally?

"Emotionally?" Brigit asked, uncomprehending.

"Yes. Of course. I require a job, a place to report to, colleagues, that sort of thing," Alexis said. "I'm very fond of my students. Most of them, anyway.... Why are you looking at me like that?"

"I wouldn't have thought you felt that way."

"But why not? Why shouldn't I feel that way?"

Brigit kissed him, and stroked his hair, and could not think how to reply. She believed he was telling the truth now—he spoke so simply, so directly—and yet it did not seem quite possible: Alexis Kessler saying such things?

"Don't you like the idea of a community too?" Alexis asked. "The sort of thing Oliver makes speeches about. ... Of course I can't stand most of the people at Woodslee but the idea is superb and I have a kind of Platonic belief in...in some sort of essence.... Don't you feel the same way? I've given up on my family, I don't believe in marrying and having children, but I think there's something very real about people sharing certain values, certain beliefs—The community of art, of artists—Don't you agree?"

It had not occurred to Brigit in quite that way but she supposed that, yes, she did agree. When the frightening bouts of exhaustion had overtaken her—and now, now that she and Alexis were lovers, they had nearly stopped, thank God—it was the knowledge that she had to be somewhere, she had to meet with colleagues or students, she *had* to get up and get dressed and be presentable that drew her up, gave her the energy, however feeble, to return to the world. And she did like that world. She complained, like everyone else; but she liked it; she knew who she was in it; it may have saved her life more than once without her conscious knowledge.

But it was not a world, a community, in which Brigit felt altogether comfortable. Nor did Alexis. They could not speak openly of their feelings to their colleagues, since everything they said—especially if it was critical or abrasive or mildly "interesting"—was repeated and magnified and distorted. If Brigit expressed temporary despair over her marriage or her writing ("Your writing?" Alexis asked in surprise. "I would have thought your writing came easily to you, that's the impression you give...."), in a few days everyone in Woodslee would be saying she was suicidal, or had even attempted suicide; more than once people approached her on the street or in the supermarket or in the university library with expressions of sober restraint, even of heartfelt compassion, wanting to take her hand to console her to give her courage or—or whatever—she had no idea what was going on most of the time. ("But I'd always heard that you did things impulsively, even bluntly," Alexis said, "even...well, brutally. That *is* the impression you give.") And of course her colleagues were quick to detect, and to resent, any indication of superiority on her part. ("Oh, we're both hated because we consider ourselves superior to Woodslee," Alexis laughed, yawning. "But what can we do, my love?—we *are* superior.") On the contrary, Brigit said emphatically, she was rather in awe of her colleagues, especially in the English department—the compromises they had made with mediocrity, both professionally and domestically. There wasn't a man in the department, with the possible exception of two or three of the senior staff members and Stanislaus Chung, who wasn't really bright—even brilliant—or had been, certainly, at one time: Brigit knew, she had made a point of reading their books and essays and reviews. She *wanted* to know and to admire her colleagues. But something had
120

happened to them. Something very sad seemed to have happened. In mid-career most of them had simply ...stopped. Stopped reading widely, stopped thinking; stopped writing anything of more than routine academic importance. Certainly there were exceptions: Gowan Vaughan-Jones, Lewis himself, one or two of the younger people. But in general their professional lives were shabby suburban gardens in which, beneath an old strip of canvas, one found a discarded child's rake; in a clump of burdock and milkweed one found an old boot; the place hummed with activity and life, the incessant jumping about of grasshoppers going nowhere. And then their domestic lives: those brain-obliterating marriages! The men had married (Brigit hoped not deliberately) women distinctly less intelligent than they; women who did not, indeed could not, share their intellectual interests—who sometimes smiled wanly and said, Oh *that?*—it's all beyond me, what he does; or *That?* All that fuss about nothing?—women whose conversations about households, vacations, children, hairdos, recipes, local scandals, induced in Brigit jaw-wrenching yawns she tried gallantly to swallow. She *liked* these women, some of them were truly fine people, like Marilyn Byrne, and Mina Housley, and poor Faye Seidel...but she simply could not tolerate their company, and she sensed their dislike and disapproval of her life.

"You're lonely," Alexis said bluntly. "Like me."

"Is that it?" Brigit said, charmed.

She had fallen in love with Alexis because he was so vibrant, so attractive, so impetuous, so gentle: when he had kissed her, that first time, in her kitchen, he had half-lifted her from her chair and stood above her, gripping her thin shoulders, daringly, yet almost brotherly, with a physical compassion she no longer associated with men. How can people say you are sardonic and flippant and arrogant, Brigit wanted to protest to him, burying her face in his neck, hugging his sides, when you are one of the most...the most congenial people I have ever met.... His sexual grace, his sexual agility, were far less astonishing than his simple frank unanticipated friendliness.

They lay about the hotel room, and then showered together, and dressed, and went for a long walk, up to the mountain and along the Rue des Pins, and back around again to Sherbrooke; they stopped at the Ritz-Carlton and had a late lunch and several drinks; gripping their fingers together tightly, they hurried back to their room, kissing in the elevator, flushed and breathless and apprehensive. It was all so new; it seemed to Brigit experimental and provisionary; she supposed she was opening herself to a great hurt, but there was no time, she hadn't even the breath to draw back, to contemplate....

Alexis reminded her of no one. No other man she'd known, let alone loved.

And then there was his striking appearance: that beautiful face.

And his slim, well-proportioned body; his modest but strong shoulder and arm muscles; his hard thighs; his slender pale hands and feet. (Which were not grimy. Which were clean and nearly as soft as her own.) She kissed him and caressed him and stroked him almost with a sort of greed, a hunger she hadn't known was in her.

When he told her she was a very attractive woman, when he insisted upon the fact, fairly laughing at her refusal to believe him, she felt, queerly, as if she were deceiving him: as if someday he would find her out and no longer care for her. And at the same time she could see herself drifting into vanity...outfitting herself, acquiring the right make-up, the tricky little accessories, that might flatter her appearance and make her seem younger. "But what I really love about you," she said, quite sincerely, lying with him naked on the oversized magisterial bed, "is the fact that I can talk to you about anything, and you don't judge."

"Of course I don't judge," Alexis said. "At least not *you,* Brigit."

Their intimacy encouraged her: she began to speak, hesitantly at first, of her writing—which was after all the center of her life, or had been before she met him. Her novel. Her wretched novel. Which she had been working on for years, and which still seemed so far from completion....She had labored at two separate drafts, and there were drawers filled with unused notes, hundreds of sheets of paper, brain-swirlings scribbled at four in the morning that were unintelligible at dawn and never again read but stuffed in the drawer along with everything else, all a great heartbreaking mess. Virginia Woolf noted in her diary that her work, her ceaseless mental activity, was like a strip of pavement over an abyss; Brigit felt she knew what the metaphor meant. The work was a triumph over despondency, but if the work itself became despondency, how could one be saved...?

She wanted desperately to finish the novel, she told Alexis. Yet she couldn't write. It was easier to plan course lectures, to reread material she'd read a dozen times already, it was far easier to invite students into her office for "conferences" on their "major papers," no matter if they took up hours of her time drifting onto personal subjects: their parents, their current loves, their gripes about other professors. Even correcting examinations was oddly pleasurable. It was so definite, so real, so pragmatic, it had immediate consequences, it was after all a part of her professional responsibility....Teaching was addictive, and so was the busyness, the fuss, the exaggeration of small things that characterizes the academic life.

But why can't you finish your novel? Alexis asked.

She had no idea. Her very desperation got in her way, made her anxious, weak....The novel was to evoke the Norfolk of her childhood and girlhood, it was to be a feat of memory, an homage to the past, not sharply critical and analytical like her first two novels, but subtler...slower, less pointed, flowing and sprawling like life itself...something generous, something complete. A celebration, as St. Dennis said.

A novel about childhood, Alexis murmured.

Well—not really about childhood. About much more than that.

Alexis poured them both drinks. Straight Scotch, very powerful, very soothing.

After a while he said he hadn't any feelings about his own childhood. He was inclined to think all that

123

was overrated—the so-called gifts of perception children possess. And then it had been so boring, to be watched constantly; to be under the thumbs of two adults from whom you had to hide, naturally, your most important thoughts. His parents were conventional people, his father was an executive with Prudential Life, his mother an amateur pianist and organizer of musical groups, that sort of thing. He rarely thought of them and they had long since stopped despairing over him.

At this point in his life, Alexis said, the music that excited him was more intellectual than emotional. Memories of his childhood in Waterbury, Connecticut, meant nothing to him because they had no application to his work. Anyway, he was temperamentally inhospitable to nostalgia—what was nostalgia but a sentimental slander on reality? "Music has had enough emotion, it has been drenched in emotion," he said.

"You sound very pragmatic," Brigit said slowly.

"I am nothing if not pragmatic."

"And yet everyone thinks.... You give the impression of...."

"Yes, what?" Alexis asked sharply.

But Brigit could not say. That Alexis Kessler was thought to be reckless, slovenly, lazy, debauched, willfully wasteful of his talent and energy and youth.... It seemed no longer possible to her that anyone should really believe such nonsense. Brigit laughed and drank her Scotch and refused to consider it. Instead she asked him about his boyhood. If not his childhood, his boyhood. Tell me, she begged, about the first girl you fell in love with.

"Girl?" said Alexis calmly.

No, it was boy; a boy of seventeen or eighteen; an assistant conductor at the New England Conservatory, a prodigy, sallow-skinned, already balding, with a pinched, meticulous expression, whose smiles were cataclysmic—Alexis was eleven or twelve at the time and lived for those smiles. Sick with love for the better part of a year, he was, and though it was a small lifetime ago he remembered vividly the humiliations and ecstasies of that infatuation; he dreamed of the boy sometimes, even now.... What had become of him? Oh, a quite ordinary career, a conductor with a Midwestern symphony orchestra, St. Louis and then Kansas City and then Alexis had lost track of him, no longer interested. He, Alexis, had been the real prodigy, a pampered darling, a little prince, and it had always seemed to him, in the years that followed, quite likely that the young man had been attracted to him...but neither had dared approach the other.

"If I saw him now I wouldn't even bother to cross the street to him," Alexis said slowly. He shivered. "It's extraordinary, isn't it, how we change. How passion fades...."

Brigit's first love was a boy of about fifteen whose father was involved in city and county politics, as Brigit's father had been; she must have been twelve years old at the time she fell in love with him. He was a high-school student, she a seventh-grader. Ludicrous and pitiful, her fantasies of him, her prowling after him downtown as he walked along, oblivious to her, in a group of boys his own age. His name had been Ronnie. Ronnie Brooker. (That name had the power, still, to make her pulse jump—for a moment.) He and his friends had been loud and rather homely and exceptionally profane, even obscene; they had shouted filthy words at girls and at one another, laughing maniacally, and Brigit had excused it all—hadn't understood it, perhaps. She had loved him for over a year. He had worn a certain maroon jacket, a canvas jacket with *Norfolk JC's* stitched in gold on the back, and she had loved that jacket, had looked for it in the crowds that milled about the high-school steps and on the streets, on Saturdays and at the roller rink, and....She laughed, hiding her face in her hands. It had been hideous, that infatuation, but also rather wonderful. She had never forgotten him. Whenever she went back home she looked his name up in the telephone directory and checked his address and it was always the same—he'd married a girl in his senior class, they had several children who were probably grown up now, he didn't know the name "Brigit Stott" at all. He knew nothing of her, nothing.

But the most important person of her girlhood, Brigit said, wasn't that boy; it was a girl named Louellen. They had known each other from first grade to tenth grade, they had been best friends for nine years, and now—so many years later—Brigit sometimes dreamed of her. For a long time she had simply forgotten her. The youngest of seven children, her father an alcoholic, a former miner, always on relief, her mother—Louellen's poor mother—an employee at one of the canning factories. Her six brothers and sisters always in trouble. Louellen had been skinny and big-eyed and surprisingly funny, and though Brigit's parents had known nothing of the shoplifting expeditions the girls had gone on—mainly to Woolworth's and Grant's—they had sensed something dangerous in Louellen, and had disapproved of her family because of their poverty; so they hadn't encouraged Brigit to invite Louellen home. And they had never allowed Brigit to spend the night with Louellen. But the girls had been closer than sisters, they had loved each other very much, had exchanged innumerable gifts—purses, scarves, games, cheap bracelets—and were known to be inseparable. One Christmas, Brigit spent five dollars on Louellen, an extraordinary sum; she bought Louellen a pair of fur-lined gloves. Louellen in turn gave Brigit a topaz ring that had belonged to her grandmother. Topaz! The setting was rather cheap but the stone was genuine. When the parents discovered it they had wanted Brigit to return it to Louellen, but Louellen wouldn't take it back, and Brigit had not known what to do. There were many telephone calls. There was a great deal of weeping. The Stotts were upset and vaguely insulted, and Louellen's parents were angry. In the end Brigit had been allowed to keep the ring but she had not worn it, for fear of losing it, and for years it remained in her mother's bureau drawer, untouched; it was probably still there. "Sometimes it seems to me," Brigit said, "that I've never had another friend who meant that much to me. Something happened to Louellen's mother when we were in the tenth grade and the family was broken up—she went to Baltimore to live with a married sister—and we wrote for a while but I never saw her again. Sometimes I dream I'm back in Norfolk, I'm a girl again, and Louellen is somewhere near, and it's very important that I find her—but I can't find her. We're at school, we're downtown, we're lost. I don't know where to look. I call her name but she doesn't answer. In the dream I start to cry, I make a wailing sound—like the wailing of an animal—I'm horrified by the sound of my own voice—but—but nothing happens, Louellen doesn't come. I wake up gasping for air. My body seems to be going through the motions of crying, of sorrow—but I don't know why—I don't understand it. I'm so upset that it takes me an hour or more to get back to sleep," she said, wiping at her eyes. "I really don't understand it."

Alexis seemed touched. "You wake up crying?"

"It's terrible," Brigit said. Then she laughed, not wanting to sound so plaintive. "But it hasn't happened for a while."

"I don't think I've cried for years," Alexis said slowly. "It must be something of an accomplishment.... Crying over a girl you haven't seen for so long, crying over a childhood friend: yes, it's an accomplishment. I've never cried over a friend. I don't even know what the word means: friend. Friendship. There have been lovers, of course; I've cried over them. But not for a long time and even while I was crying I think I knew how pointless it was, how futile and self-serving. Weeping for little Alexis, who can't have his own way all the time...."

"You sound awfully hard," Brigit said uneasily.

"I'm not hard, not at all," Alexis said. He sat up and reached for his cigarettes. The new silver ring glinted on the third finger of his right hand, so large as to nearly cover his knuckle. He smelled of perspiration and cologne. "I'm realistic. I'm neutral. As you say, I'm pragmatic.... I'm much older than you are, Brigit."

St. Dennis in his dark three-piece suit, his white hair seeming to float softly about his face, his voice a little weaker now: a wry, convoluted poem about love, written decades ago, set in a rundown resort hotel in Southampton. Crabbed, cruel, jarring, astringent. Love's

127

nostalgia. Yearning for the dark, for dark places, for paradise, for the mythic center of Schopenhauer's vast dream of a universe in which dreamers are dreamed and in turn dream—*must* dream or become extinct. The audience is quick to laugh at the satirical lines and Brigit laughs with them though her body wants to weep, her body is protesting, she is in love and cannot bear a slander upon love, not now, not now. And yet St. Dennis is witty and wise and she too will applaud him.

...Bucking, heaving, straining. Her heartbeat ferocious. She grasps at him, clutches at him. It cannot be happening to her, not after so long, so many years, she isn't certain she really wants it to happen to her: yet she is drawn irresistibly forward, her mouth open and twisted, saliva running down her chin. She loves him, she clutches at his hair, his shoulders, his back, she beats at him with a fist that breaks open, helpless, the fingers spread.... It cannot be happening. (Stanley, who loved her, who protested how he loved her, weeping as she wept, bewildered at his own cruelty, unable to comprehend his sudden outbursts of rage, derision, mockery, despair—Stanley saying she was tight-bodied, too shy, still virginal in her imagination, always resisting him—didn't she know how he loved her, how he wanted only to be certain she loved him?) With Alexis she is open and helpless and raw and heaving and it frightens her to know she must seem ugly to him, her mouth gaping, her eyes dilated, but she cannot stop, she does not want to stop, he embraces her tightly as if unaware of her terror. She is about to lose control of herself. Panicked, she falls back; she wants to escape; she does not trust him. She does not know him. Someone, a man, a stranger, a lover or a husband...someone is making love to her and she is frightened, she does not know him, does not know what will happen to her. With one part of her mind she dismisses it all as absurd: she has sloughed off any interest in men, in love, in enduring bouts of lovemaking and submitting herself to another person's judgment. She does not care for anyone's opinion of her and does not want to care. She is thirty-eight years old, she has been married, she has

128

lived with a man for years and now lives alone and prefers to live alone and is happiest in the early morning when, alone, she looks out the window of her sixth-floor apartment and sees the sky lightening, sees the first of the birds—sparrows and juncos mainly—picking about the seed on her tiny balcony; she walks through the apartment, alone, rejoicing in her aloneness, she makes coffee, she considers working at her desk, she wonders if perhaps—if—perhaps today—if she might have better luck with her novel—if she dare attempt it—Alone, rejoicing in the quiet, walking about half-dressed, feeding the cat and unembarrassed at talking to it, isn't this Brigit who is independent of others' judgment, isn't this Brigit Stott as she knows herself from the inside, isn't this her truest self...?

With one part of her mind she dismisses rudely even the proffered love of Alexis Kessler: she knows he is going to hurt her badly and she wants no new pain, not now. With another part of her mind, however, she is afraid that something will happen to her one day when she is alone, there is an overbright insistent elation to her aloneness, her emphatic independence; she is guilty of something—what?—and will be punished. Though a day might begin marvelously, she is always in danger of being overcome by mid-afternoon by one of those spells of fatigue that are so sudden and so profound as to seem, almost, blackouts. Sleep during the day isn't soothing but very disturbing. She knows there is something wrong with it, with her, she dreads the heavy drugged deathly naps, she sinks into sleep as if into the grave and has no faith, really, that she will wake again: and at the moment of sleep it sometimes crosses her mind that she does not care. Quick, fleeting, teasing, cruel. So cruel. You drink too much, her mother might say; Stanley might say, aren't you taking too many pills...? You're suicidal. You always were. Die, why don't you, I promise not to interfere, you know you can trust me. Trust me. You know you can trust me.... Waking so brightly but without any appetite, alone, guilty and uneasy and happy in a perverse way, filled with a profound sense of unearned pleasure if, among the birds on her balcony, she saw a cardinal or a grosbeak or even a jay—there was a jay in the neighborhood with a broken leg, poor doomed creature flopping about and flying with difficulty—but unable to eat, unable even to think of food for most of the day: so she drank coffee and smoked cigarettes, went out to teach her classes or attend meetings, or stayed home on the days she didn't teach, driven by a peculiar inexplicable energy, alert and attentive and perhaps a little edgy, hoping to avoid the sudden weariness that called to her mind's eye the instant of collapse of a piece of paper dropped upon a fire—at first whole, white, complete, then scorched and blackened, and then, suddenly and irreparably, overcome by flame and destroyed. There were days when she began to feel hungry only around eight o'clock. Even then she prepared a meal only with reluctance and an obscure sense of resentment, as if she were being forced to cook for someone she despised. She often made scrambled eggs, impatiently; the eggs scorched and stuck to the pan and she cried aloud in vexation. If her black silky longhaired cat brushed against her legs at such times she kicked it away. Damn it! Damn you! But then she would be suddenly ravenous, she would sit at the kitchen table and eat the eggs and two or three pieces of toast, her hands fairly shaking, her eyes watering, she would eat the entire meal in ten minutes after having eaten nothing in twenty-four hours; then suddenly she would feel bloated and sick, she would rise from the table, revulsed, again resentful, she would stagger to the sink and put the dishes and the pan in it to soak overnight, now she was reeling with exhaustion and wanted only to go to bed: nothing mattered except sleep. Her stomach was bloated, hard, her brain was emptied of blood, she went to bed and waited for sleep to overtake her at last, violent and merciful as a hammer blow. It seemed to her at such times that she was all stomach—the tight, heavy mass of food in her was all that remained of her, all that was vital and living. Her name, her personality, her work, her fate?—nothing mattered.

But Alexis mattered, Alexis matters; she does not dare tell him of these peculiar habits of hers though she has confessed other eccentricities (as he has confessed charming eccentricities of his own: a fanatic's sense of perfection in his work, for one thing). Since that night in September when they became lovers Brigit has believed herself changed, she is optimistic about changing, about becoming more normal, and she is not a person to take pride in quirky, self-destructive behavior.... He matters to her; he matters very much. With another man she would be self-conscious, but with Alexis there is no consciousness of self, there seem at times to be no self, no selves, at all. "I love you," he says, and she repeats, "I love you," and they clutch at each other, blind, eager, childlike, hopeful. Again, again, again. The first time they made love Brigit could not believe that it was happening to her, she wished to stand aside in despair, in hilarity, in awe, as she had sometimes stood aside with her husband, unable to remain in her body, unable to subordinate herself to him, to his strenuous exercises, his vexed and arduous will; but she found herself kissing and embracing and loving Alexis, absurdly grateful for him, astonished at his beauty—that a man should be so handsome, and not stupid!—she could not quite believe in him even as she loved him, writhing with pleasure beneath his body. No. Yes. No. She is terrified of losing control of herself; she is terrified that she will not lose control but will remain behind, unchanged. She knows she has felt pleasure before and has not been destroyed and yet it seems to her, each time, that she must stop—must not continue. That flurry of pleasure, spiraling upward suddenly and carrying her with it and throwing her body into convulsions: she will not endure it, she wants desperately to endure it, she clutches at her lover and cries aloud of her love for him, the madness of her love for him.

A horrible childlike wailing—she hears it, it fills the room, it cannot be disowned.

Afterward he wipes the tears from her face, sometimes kisses them away. But does not ask why she cries and why, afterward, she is so stricken, so mute.

Woodslee University, founded in 1848, with a chapter of Phi Beta Kappa established in 1879, is a private, richly endowed institution famous in the East for its high tuition, its liberal arts and fine arts departments, and its academic rigor; though much has been made in recent years of a lowering of standards. Students rejected at Harvard, Yale, and Princeton routinely come to Woodslee, as they come to Cornell, or the University of Pennsylvania, or Boston University, or even the state universities of New York. There are approximately six thousand undergraduates, two thousand graduate students, and a negligible number of part-time students. The majority are from New York City and its suburbs, though there are a number from the Midwest, and from California; there is a considerable foreign-student population. The university was built just to the west of the small town of Woodslee, New York, on the Powhatan River, and it covers more than three hundred acres of land, bounded on the east by Lake Champlain and on the west, irregularly, by the Adirondack Mountains. Much of the land is hilly and densely wooded and impenetrable. Woodslee is famous for its architectural beauty, the ferocity of its winters (porch thermometers in the area are equipped to register thirty degrees below zero), a certain ascetic zealousness among its most vocal faculty members and alumni, and a sense of uneasy privilege among its students, only minimally eroded by the "democratizing" influences of the sixties. It is an expensive school, how can one deny the fact?—despite a number of scholarship students (blacks, "the culturally deprived") it belongs to affluent America, and does that America justice.

The campus is impressive even to visitors who are not easily impressed. They marvel at the uniform Greek Revival architecture, the buildings made of limestone and granite from a once-rich quarry in nearby Kittyboro; and at the small marble chapel with an Italian rose window of stained glass; and the many graveled walks and curving graveled tree-lined drives; the old bell tower; the old Administration Building atop a steep hill; Brandford Hall with its innumerable columns; the new limestone-and-glass library, built in 1971 at a considerable (and controversial) cost, several hundred thousand dollars above the builder's original estimate; the palatial student union, overlooking a gully and a waterfall; Kerr Theater with its sweeping buttresses and startling peacock-blue glass; dormitories that resemble elegant old apartment buildings, on the outside at least; dining halls all plate glass and Italian terra cotta; the president's neo-Georgian home that rivals the White House itself in restrained splendor, and is in a far more attractive setting with the Adirondacks in the background, and blue spruce and enormous oaks and elms on all sides, and a garden of roses and ornamental trees and statuary nearby, open to the public. Even the graduate students' housing on the far side of campus, over by the physical education complex and the security division, is fairly attractive. There are bicycle paths, tennis courts, small lakes, granite benches, a monument commemorating the Battle of Powhatan in 1777. *Attendance at Woodslee University is a privilege that can be revoked at any time,* incoming freshmen read in their orientation week booklets.

A place of worship, Brigit Stott thought uneasily when she was first driven through the campus.

The 1977 census showed a population of approximately twenty-three thousand for the town of Woodslee, down several hundred from the previous census.

There has been an unemployment problem in the area now for some years: one of the textile mills was forced to close in the late sixties. The town is small and undistinguished; there is a fairly large park on the river with a Revolutionary War monument at its center; the new Bank of America is an impressive though rather small building; there are a single movie theater, a single downtown hotel, and a few motels at the edge of town, along Highway 9. There are a number of small factories—paper pulp; women's and girls' sweaters; fish packing; shoes. There is a single high school. Near the interstate expressway to the east is a new shopping mall—Powhatan Hills—and the usual gasoline stations and drive-in restaurants and motels, and several subdivisions featuring small modestly priced "colonials" and "ranch-type" houses.

Very few of the university faculty or administrators live on the east side. The most attractive part of town is just north of the university and across the river, Phoenix Heights. There, lots are wooded and sloping and usually quite large, lanes are unpaved, houses are occasionally hidden from sight behind massive stands of spruce and Scotch pine, there are fieldstone walls, there is a sense of privacy and great worth. The Byrnes live on Fairway Drive; their property is adjacent to the enormous lot owned by Judge Conroy, now retired, a prominent member of the Board of Governors of Woodslee University. (The Conroy house, a neo-Georgian mansion, was built in 1881 by one of the mill owners.) On the golf course of the Phoenix Hills Country Club there is an amazing house—owned by a Woodslee attorney, for whom it was especially designed by Frank Lloyd Wright—or one of his associates—consisting of numerous layers or slabs of limestone punctuated by panels of glass that appear to be blue-tinted; on their first Sunday drive north of town Sandra and Ernest Jaeger were much taken by this house, though Sandra came to feel, on subsequent drives, that it did not have the dignity of other homes in the area.

Just to the east of the university campus is another excellent residential area of two-and three-storied homes, most of them brick; it is here that the majority of the university people live. There are a number of extraordinary Victorian houses in the neighborhood, three or four Greek-revival houses, even an octagon-

134

shaped house with a veranda circling it on its second floor, on Colfax Avenue, owned by Dr. Trevor of the fine arts department; the Trevors' house is of course coveted by everyone in the area. On Linwood Avenue a few houses down from the apartment building where Brigit Stott lives there is an exquisite Cape Cod, owned by the Haases; around the corner on Strathmore there is a possibly ugly but impressive old Victorian mansion with innumerable narrow windows and queer jutting angles and slopes of roof that appear to be rotting and a tiny sun porch whose window, facing the street, is completely clotted with plants whose leaves and tendrils seem to be growing flat against the glass—a home owned by the widow of the former Dean of Humanities, a woman who speaks of putting the house on the market every spring but then unaccountably, and maddeningly, never does: the house is so large, however, and the heating bills so high (it is speculated), that she will probably not be able to hold out much longer. At the other end of Strathmore is the Seidels' house, also generally coveted. Built in 1910, it is sprawling and asymmetrical and grandiose, a mixture of styles, Victorian and Tudor, with the customary small windows, and spires and peaks and turrets and stained glass in the stairwell, and wide oak archways, and high ceilings; a child's nightmare of a house, vaguely suggestive of Germanic fairy tales, its downstairs rooms always a little dark. The foyer, slate-floored, is overlarge and always chilly; it is impressive, however, like the wide staircase leading down to it. Faye Seidel has placed a cobbler's bench just inside the door, and there is an antique coat rack with a cloudy mirror, and an umbrella stand picked up cheaply at a country auction—covered in deerskin, it is something of a curiosity. The house is agreeably shabby. Its rooms are smaller than one might suspect because of the wide archways and the oversized closets, and Lewis's study—just to the right of the front door—is almost tiny. Crammed with bookshelves, it is messy and shadowy, like a cave; it gives an air of being comfortable, however, and protective. The bathrooms were renovated when the Seidels bought the house some time ago—amazing, it has been fifteen years now—and the kitchen was completely redone, so that guests are moderately surprised, walking from the living room and the dining room into a kitchen of gray-colored surfaces, orange and lime counters, a floor covered with something slick as plastic, walls covered with tile suggestive of the Southwest. The stove and refrigerator are olive green; the big unsanded cypress table looks like a butcher's block; there is always an air about the Seidels' kitchen, during parties, of desperate good-natured merriment, a messiness that is somehow reassuring, as if part of the festivity.

It is partly the house, it is partly Lewis's marvelous exuberance, that account for the success of the Seidels' parties. They give a party in the fall, generally, and in the spring; occasionally they give a New Year's Eve party. Lewis has estimated that the house can hold one hundred guests if they spread out into all the downstairs rooms. A few parties have become legendary, having lasted throughout the night and into the morning; there are admiring tales still in circulation of long drinking bouts and dazzling repartee at the Seidels' when John Berryman came to Woodslee to give a poetry reading and stayed at the Seidels', and Lewis invited most of the university community to a party in Berryman's honor. There is always praise for Lewis's generosity with liquor and for the food Faye serves, which is more lavish and imaginative than the food offered by people—like the Housleys and the Hochbergs—who have considerably more money than Faye and Lewis.

Lewis loves parties. He is loud, merry, euphoric; it is only 9:15 and a half-dozen couples have already arrived, all friends of his, friends and colleagues, grateful to be invited to his party for Albert St. Dennis. He expects the old man himself at any moment: Oliver Byrne is to drive him over.

After the disturbing rumors of St. Dennis's ill health, the gossip about his drinking and his quarrel with someone in the administration and his threats to quit...what a marvelous surprise, the old man's performance tonight! Everyone is impressed. Everyone is pleased. The doorbell rings and Lewis hurries to the

136

foyer, but his son, Harry, is already opening the door—who is it?—ah, just Gladys Fetler, pink-cheeked, her raincoat and plastic rain hat streaming wet. "You didn't walk all the way, did you?" Lewis cries, as much for the pleasure of hearing his own raised voice as for anything else; he takes Gladys's cold hand and grips it hard and introduces her to his son, who is seventeen, long-haired and shy, and already an inch taller than Lewis.

9:20. 9:25. The rain has turned to sleet; people hurry up the Seidels walk, stamp their feet on the porch and in the foyer, shake their umbrellas, exclaim in high elated voices that driving conditions will be very bad tonight and it's only the first week of November.... George and Mina Housley, both out of breath. Joe and Mona Cuffe. The Bannons. Excited, Lewis shows them into the living room, asks them what drinks they would like. (There is a bar set up in one corner of the dining room, near the archway.) He is pleased to see them, pleased to see everyone. His friends. His colleagues. He squeezes Brad Keough's arm in passing and asks how he is and how he liked the reading?—excellent, wasn't it? Lewis's gray-red hair rises from his ruddy face in exuberant spurts; wide creasing smiles ray across his face, distending his nostrils. The time? Only 9:25. He is very excited. He has been planning this party for weeks.

Already rather warm, he takes off his jacket and gives it to Faye to hang up; he is wearing a dark blue shirt of some thick, coarse texture, rather stylish, and a cream-colored necktie, and a new pair of trousers. He carries a drink and a cigarette in his left hand, so that his right hand is free. He squeezes someone's arm, he slips his own arm around a friend's shoulder and leans into a conversation—do you people all know one another?—does anyone need a drink?—more ice? What did you think of St. Dennis—wasn't the old boy superb tonight? Gowan Vaughan-Jones, in a peculiar muddy-green corduroy jacket that is too large for him, asks Lewis his opinion of St. Dennis's new poems and Lewis can't ease away—Matt Ryerson is standing there, blocking the doorway—and so he lists the qualities in the new poems that struck him as admirable, and those that struck him as egregious; as he has told Gowan in the past, the poems of St. Dennis's he most approves of are those gray-lit sardonic *Motorway* sonnets, muted, mean, defiantly mundane: English poets are only good, Lewis declares loudly, when they satirize their depleted impoverished ludicrous tottering empire. The new poems were moving, of course, and courageous, but the risks were too much for the old man—didn't Gowan agree?—no?—but he must agree the subject of bereavement is dangerous, and that St. Dennis—despite his characteristic control of language and those brave brittle tricks he has mastered—faltered once or twice and sank into sentimentality—?

The doorbell rings. Lewis excuses himself and pushes through the crowd. But Harry has opened the door and Faye is greeting Pete Springer, who is alone, and Lewis rushes forward to shake his old friend's hand, not wanting him to see he's disappointed. Pete is a friend of ten or twelve years, a colleague Lewis's own age, recently divorced; his breath smells of alcohol. What did he think of the reading, Lewis asks. Pete shakes his head, embarrassed, and says he hadn't been able to make the reading; had been busy with something else. . . . Up the walk come two couples, at first Lewis can't even recognize them, then in the porchlight they turn into those new people, those young people, the Jaegers and the Swansons: he greets them himself and urges them inside, wants to make them feel at home, asks if they had any difficulty finding the house?—people often did. The girls are both very attractive. They are so young, and so eager to smile! The dark-haired one with the faint mustache on her upper lip and the lovely brown eyes is complimenting him and Faye on their house while she struggles out of her coat—a full bosom, full hips, a strong perfumy odor, a dress of purple zigzags that fits her snugly; the other one, Sandra, the blonde whom Vivian Hochberg has spoken of to Lewis, gives him a dazzling smile, her lower lip caught in her teeth, her eyes on a level with his. She is wearing an extraordinary outfit. The men in attendance—her husband and Barry Swanson—glance at her and at Lewis as if embarrassed. What is she saying?—something about St.

Dennis being a little delayed? He was evidently besieged by people after the reading, admirers and autograph seekers.... Ah, is that it? Lewis says, relieved. He has been wondering where St. Dennis is. It's already 9:30. So...is that it? He's very grateful, he tells the girl, to learn that St. Dennis is all right, what with the sleet and the bad driving.... Would she like a drink? Why didn't they all follow him into the living room? It might be easier for them to introduce themselves to his guests, but let him make them drinks first, what would Sandra like, why didn't she just hang onto his arm and he'd escort her through the crowd...? The girl is really striking. That platinum blond hair, that smile, that nervous flirtatious manner; and the outfit she is wearing—a tunic top, long floppy trousers made of a queer silver material, metallic and clinging. The tunic fits tightly across the girl's small hard breasts and tightly across her stomach and hips, and Lewis finds himself grinning at her body, distracted from her words, nodding emphatically. Someone bumps into him and his cigarette falls from his fingers. He stoops to pick it up, Warren Hochberg is apologizing, Lewis laughs and offers him a drink and asks where Vivian is; she *is* here, isn't she?

"Of course Vivian is here," Warren tells him. His smile is small and measured and gives the impression of turning downward. "You know she would never miss one of your parties."

Lewis escapes from Warren and uses the small lavatory beneath the stairs and goes out again to the foyer, where more people are taking off their coats. Among them are Brigit Stott and Alexis Kessler. Lewis stares at them for an instant before breaking into his hearty welcoming laugh. As he shakes hands with Kessler he senses the man's hostility; he notices that his son Harry is staring at Kessler too—having never seen a man with bleached hair and innumerable rings and filed, polished fingernails. And he smells of perfume, does he?—of cologne? Lewis would kiss Brigit on her cool cheek but he knows she may shy away, and this would embarrass everyone, so he merely squeezes her hand— quite hard, in fact—and tells her that he's delighted to see her; for some reason he had the idea she wouldn't be coming.

"Didn't I answer your invitation?" Brigit asks, opening her eyes wide as she customarily does when she is lying.

Lewis is struck by her appearance. It is Brigit Stott his old friend and colleague—and yet it isn't Brigit, it is a strikingly attractive young woman, far younger than her age; she is almost beautiful. Her eyes are darkly emphatic, her lipstick is an unobtrusive pale fleshy-pink, there is something arrogant and radiant about her very being. So she is in love! And how obvious it is! Lewis would guffaw incredulously, but he is too moved, too strangely disconcerted, for hadn't there been from the very first a sort of understanding between him and Stott....From their first lively meeting at the party in New York, when Lewis had penetrated her husband's defense....

Brigit and Alexis. Lovers, pretending (in public) to be no more than friends. Lewis is tempted to wink at them and nudge them in the ribs. *He* knows. Why dissemble with *him?*

(The rumors Lewis has heard! For weeks tales have made the rounds of the university, coiling and doubling back on themselves, growing ever richer, ever more scandalous. The Stott woman and that Kessler walking brazenly along the river with their arms around each other; Kessler, never before seen in the Humanities Building, emerging flushed and disheveled from Stott's office on the second floor, carrying an armload of books for a prop. It was said that in a resort hotel in Sarasota, where the two had escaped for a weekend, Stott emptied a drink in Kessler's face, and the resulting brawl—in the hotel's elegant cocktail lounge—brought not only the hotel's detective but a city patrolman as well. A young instructor in the music department stopped by at Kessler's studio apartment to ask Kessler to return some music he'd borrowed (Kessler is notorious for neglecting to return anything he has borrowed, particularly money), but there was no answer when he rang the bell, and as he was about to leave he heard—he is *certain* he heard—a woman shouting angrily inside:

Brigit Stott's voice without question. It has been said that the two of them smoke hashish together. Alexis flies back and forth to New York frequently (on an admirer's borrowed credit card), where he is supplied with hashish, and even cocaine; and the Stott woman has been sniffling of late, hasn't she, and is often red-eyed when she meets her classes—aren't the symptoms obvious? A depraved, debauched pair. Really quite demoralizing for the community. And what their impressionable students must think—! Lewis heard from two different sources on the same Monday morning that Brigit's former husband—or are they still married?—tried to break into Brigit's apartment over the weekend, when Kessler was there. In one version Brigit fired her revolver into the door (it is said she carries a handgun everywhere, in her purse, though no one has actually seen it; and once, when Lewis wandered into her office next to his and she wasn't there, he took the opportunity to glance casually through her purse and was mildly disappointed to come upon only a much-worn wallet of imitation leather, some crumpled tissues, a comb with broken teeth, a cheap dime-store compact, a lipstick in a plastic tube, and loose pennies) and Stanley Fifield fled; in the other version he actually succeeded in getting the door off its hinges, but police were called. Lewis has also heard that Brigit and Alexis are planning to resign their appointments at Woodslee and elope to Greece; or is it Northern Africa; or Mexico? He has heard (this by way of his wife, who heard it from Vivian Hochberg at the Faculty Wives' Association luncheon the other day) that Brigit and Alexis are pursuing Albert St. Dennis shamelessly...dropping in at his apartment, inviting themselves over, doing errands for him. Lewis was a little upset to hear this; he half-wondered if he should warn St. Dennis that they were plotting to befriend him for selfish reasons....)

He steers them into the living room, one hand touching lightly against Kessler's back, the other gripping Brigit's arm at the elbow. He asks Brigit how she enjoyed the reading, eying her closely, curiously, believing that he sees in her a certain arrogant confidence, the result, no doubt, of her alliance with Kessler. Lovers, the two of them! *Them*. He makes Brigit a drink and Kessler makes his own, ignoring Lewis's friendly chatter, actually turning away as if he were unaware of his host; the effeminate bastard. Lewis glances at his wrist watch without seeing the time and, nervous, knowing himself too excited, continues to address Brigit though he senses she wants to edge away from him. St. Dennis is going to be a few minutes late for the party, he tells Brigit. Did she know—there is a reporter here from the Albany *Post* to interview St. Dennis and take a few pictures? He's over in the corner by the Haases and he had expressed the wish to meet her too, he'd heard of her novels, wondered if....Brigit says something Lewis can't make out, she has a bad habit of mumbling, and in this din it's impossible to hear her; he stoops and inclines his head toward her and she draws back, the bitch, with a foolish little laugh; at this moment Faye approaches, harassed and heavier than Lewis recalls, in a blue silk hostess gown, with a plea that he come to the foyer and help out—poor Leslie Cullendon needs help.

Lewis finishes his drink and sets the glass down. Leslie Cullendon. Leslie...? He doesn't remember having invited the Cullendons.

9:40. The house is crowded. There are guests in his study and in the hall, sitting on the stairs, Rhoda Taylor of the black studies program—a willowy, very black-skinned young woman from Vassar—is laughing at something Vivian Hochberg is telling her, and both women turn as Lewis hurries past, smiling broadly as if *he* is their subject; he waves and grins in return, shoots Vivian a puzzled look, but there's no time, Barry Swanson and Todd Andress—had he invited Todd?—a student, invited to this party?—he doesn't remember—Barry and Todd are helping Leslie Cullendon with his wheelchair, lifting it up the front steps, while little feisty-chinned Babs Cullendon holds an umbrella over her husband. "Don't let go! Don't let go!" Leslie is crying drunkenly. "Watch out! Careful! *Care*-ful!"

Lewis helps; they get Leslie into the house; Bab's umbrella pokes Lewis in the cheek.

"It's stifling in here," Leslie says. "I want a drink.

Which direction is the bar? Take this fucking coat off me, Babs, for Christ's sake. I'm stifling, I tell you. I'm suffocating."

Lewis mutters something about the unexpected numbers, apologizes for the stuffiness, agrees it is quite warm—he discovers he's sweating himself, his underclothes are damp, a droplet of perspiration runs down his temple. What time is it? Where the hell is St. Dennis?...Leslie pushes his wife aside impatiently and begins to wheel himself into the living room, a thin, hunched man with a very pale face and curly shaggy hair; he would have run into Gladys Fetler if Edie Ryerson hadn't warned her and pulled her aside. Lewis exchanges a look with his wife for the first time this evening. She too is warm; her eyes are glassy. Leslie Cullendon! A dying man! Dying now for over a year, slowly, an associate professor in the department, a specialist in modern British literature whose doctoral dissertation was on James Joyce—only thirty-four years old and weakening month by month, week by week, brazenly continuing with his teaching and never absent from any departmental or committee meeting: is it possible that Lewis mistakenly put an invitation into Leslie's mailbox at the university?

"He's been drinking since lunch," Babs is saying in her whining nasal voice. "Oh, Dr. Seidel, I don't know what to do, just look at him in there, it's terrible, nobody cares, my so-called friends don't give a damn. Dr. Seidel, you know we used to be so close to the Cuffes and now Mona makes all these excuses, they just don't *want* to see Leslie any more and we used to be so close, we used to be such good friends.... Are they here? Is Mona here? Dr. Seidel, what am I going to *do?* Just look at Leslie! Pouring himself a drink! He's been drinking since lunch and he wouldn't touch his food and he's supposed to be on this high-protein diet, you know, they don't really know what's wrong with him—did I tell you?—did he tell you?—it's like multiple sclerosis but it *isn't* that—the diagnosis *isn't* multiple sclerosis—it's something to do with the spinal fluid and the brain, something about motor centers in the brain," she says, clutching at Lewis's wrist. "Dr. Seidel you don't know
143

what it's like to live with him, you just don't know, as soon as he moves away from the bar I'll make myself a drink, you needn't bother. Dr. Seidel, it's so wonderful of you to have invited us," she says, wiping at her eyes, "you just don't *know*. If it wasn't for the university keeping him on like this and letting him teach his classes and work with his students—! You just don't know, none of you *know*—Look, do you see that? Do you? Poor Leslie was heading for Brad Keough and Brad pretended not to notice and he escaped out through the kitchen—the son of a bitch!—I *saw* that myself—it's no wonder Leslie is so sensitive and paranoid about you people in the department—I *saw* that myself—"

Lewis has a fit of coughing. Little Babs makes her own drink, Lewis pours himself some Scotch in a glass, no need to bother with ice, he takes the opportunity of passing some chips and avocado dip around to his friends, nervous, keyed up, anything to escape from Babs Cullendon, a girl he had once found exceptionally pretty and had—hadn't he?—or was that another little wife?—kissed for ten or fifteen minutes very early one morning at someone's party a few years ago. He slides one arm around Matt Ryerson's broad shoulders and inclines his graying shaggy head into a conversation: Mina Housley in her piping voice, something about rent control, welfare cutbacks in the county, terrible poverty right in town a few miles away and all this agitation about expanding the highway, simply for tourists, and Woodslee wouldn't profit from tourism, as everyone knows except the politicians, who are only pretending not to know, and what about the shocking case of starvation or malnutrition reported in the paper—there may be quite a number of families as poor as that family living in the foothills—only a few miles away from the university—from this very living room—Lewis coughs and clears his throat and says that St. Dennis will be a little late; evidently quite a crowd of autograph-seekers converged on him after the reading. He sends his apologies and he'll be along any minute now....Mina Housley peers at Lewis through her bifocals. She doesn't seem to know what he's talking about, and even

Matt Ryerson smiles vaguely, and Ted Bannon cups his hand to his ear: God, you can't hear yourself think!

"Great to see you all! Great evening for a party!" Lewis cries.

He escapes, circles back to the bar—where Pete Springer has more or less taken on the responsibility of bartender—and fills up his glass again; doesn't remember having finished his last drink. So hot! All these people! Lewis's eye wanders helplessly from person to person, face to face. Colleagues. Friends. He knows them all and is fond of them all. He knows them all and....A woman throws herself backward in a spasm of laughter, colliding with Lewis so that his drink spills (fortunately not onto his trousers: onto the rug), and all the while he is nodding at Pete Springer who is complaining in a bitter monotone about his former wife. A voice nearby rises querulously: it is Stanislaus Chung of the English department, already rather drunk. Dr. Chung's quirky bad temper is legendary and Lewis wonders why he invited him...oh yes: he invited Dr. Chung because the Chungs invited *him* to a dinner party last spring. The wife is small-bodied and unobtrusive, almost pathologically shy, and consequently not much of a problem; but Chung himself is bristly, loud and whining when drunk, really quite unpredictable. He has joined Matt Ryerson and the others, a stocky, swarthy little man with a broad grin, dressed in an ill-fitting plaid suit, curiously asymmetrical, as if one leg were shorter than the other. Lewis is still nodding in Pete Springer's direction, numbly but enthusiastically. He is really feeling quite good. He loves parties, needs parties....He loves....

Jesus Christ: out of the corner of his eye he sees a shape in a wheelchair approaching.

In frantic haste he looks at his wrist watch without seeing the time, mumbles something to Pete, turns and hurries blindly through the dining room and into the kitchen...where Faye and Charlotte Haas are taking a large casserole out of the oven. There is an odor of something burned, scorched. Lewis stares at the clock set in the stove and sees, sickened, that it is ten minutes to ten.

145

Ten minutes to ten.

The poetry reading ended just before nine. St. Dennis had finished his last poem just before nine. Nearly an hour ago. It means: what?...Faye is nagging him, pulling at his sleeve. Has he been smoking again? How many drinks has he had? He promised, didn't he, it wouldn't be like the last time, at the Hochbergs', when he drank so much he was sick all night, and where is Mr. St. Dennis, isn't he here yet? There is a sharp line between Faye's eyebrows, a vertical crease that fascinates and repels Lewis....Charlotte Haas tells Lewis in an excited, slurred voice, one hand cupping an elbow and the other hand cupping her chin, that she'd been telling Faye about the strangest thing that had happened to her today, this morning, this was Friday, wasn't it?—it had happened just this morning. Well, Lewis knows where she and Roger live, on Linwood, doesn't he, and there's an alley out back, an alley for garbage pickup—is there an alley running behind Strathmore?—no?—anyway—anyway she was home alone as usual and happened to see, about ten A.M. it was, these two men coming along the alley walking very slowly and stooping over quite a bit—picking up something—and she watched and watched and they came to her own back yard where there's just a chain-link fence that isn't in very good condition any longer, it's quite rusted, she has asked Roger about putting in a redwood fence maybe at a height of about ten feet, and these two men looked over the fence into her back yard and for a long terrible moment she knew that something was going to happen: she *knew*. In her bathrobe and bedroom slippers, standing at the kitchen window, terrified, trembling, wondering if she should get to the telephone before it was too late—! One of the men had straggly blond hair and the other was dark and swarthy, maybe an Indian, she was quite sure he was an Indian, maybe from the reservation at DeWitt, but what was he doing down here in Woodslee?—what were these two men doing? Both wore lumberman's jackets and caps. The blond had a reddened face, the Indian was very dark, the two of them kept staring into her back yard and they weren't even talking but it was like there was a communion between them—did Lewis know what she meant?—like a scene in a movie, you know, where everything is unstated and you must *infer*—? Oh she was terrified, just terrified, because of course there was that item in the paper about the rape out by the interstate the other night in the picnic area.... Anyway the moment passed: thank God the moment passed. The men continued on down the alley and she watched until they were out of sight, going from one window to another upstairs, never so frightened in her life; what if they had decided to leap over the fence and break into the house...? They were carrying canvas bags, both of them, they were evidently scavenging around the garbage cans, but they were out of luck because the garbage wouldn't be picked up until next Tuesday and there was really little for them to take. What a terrible ten minutes Charlotte had lived through! She hopes, she says, touching Lewis's sleeve and managing a smile, she *hopes* nothing so upsetting will ever happen to her again. "It was as if my entire life flashed before me in that space of time," she says, blinking rapidly, "and I seemed to—oh, I don't know how to express it—*you* would know, Lewis, you're so articulate and—and verbal—I seemed to see how precarious and precious our lives are—our homes and our marriages—our families—And—And—It came over me like a revelation, like a vision, it was so powerful, so overwhelming: We must love one another while we have one another. I think that was it. I know I've had too much to drink, Lewis, and I've been taking antibiotics all week—fighting the flu—I know I'm not as articulate as you but I feel, I feel very deeply," she says, still touching his arm, holding his shirt sleeve, while he stares miserably into her putty-colored face, wishing only to escape, "I feel very deeply the truth of what was revealed to me and I will never, never forget—It's so precarious, you see, our homes and our marriages and the university and, oh you know, the books you men write, the meetings and the—the salaries and—Do you understand me at all, Lewis? Do you understand me at all? *We must love one another while we have one another.* We must—"

"The doorbell!" Lewis cries.

He hurries into the back hall and nearly collides with the Swanson girl, just coming out of the guest lavatory; he grips her broad shoulders and gives her a little shake, out of sheer excitement. She smiles dazedly: perhaps drunk? Lipstick on front teeth, a vague smear. Heady overripe perfume. He asks her if she's enjoying herself and she says yes, emphatically, a big happy grin, nice girl, healthy and uncomplicated and full-bodied, he asks if she and Barry know everyone, he hopes the party isn't too much of a crush for them, she says no, no, absolutely not: it's the most wonderful party she has ever been to in her life.

"You sweetheart," Lewis exclaims, squeezing her shoulder.

But when he gets to the foyer he's disappointed: Harry is taking the Bradys' coats. John and Frances Brady are old friends, very fine thoughtful cultured gentle people—John a professor of mathematics, Frances an excellent amateur cellist—but they are not, after all, Albert St. Dennis. Seeing them, Lewis groans aloud, involuntarily, but the noise from the party is such that no one hears, not even Lewis himself. He lunges forward to kiss Frances on the cheek and to shake John's hand. How good to see them, how *are* they...?

Ah, the weather! This Woodslee weather!

He leads them into the living room and excuses himself and doubles back to the front door; he stands for a few minutes on the porch, staring at the icy rain, wondering what he should do. A car's headlights—but the car continues past. What has gone wrong, where is the guest of honor? He dreads looking at his watch. Must be ten o'clock by now. The poetry reading ended at nine and an hour has passed, has slipped by, what should he do, what is going to happen...? He discovers a drink in his hand; he finishes it in one swallow. A slow dull burning sensation in his throat. A sudden attack of coughing....His son leans out the door, asks him what's wrong, doesn't he feel well? Lewis waves him away. He loves the boy—lanky awkward sweet Harry—Harry now seventeen years old, incredible as it seems—and he's grateful that his son is fond of him, as his friends' sons are not fond of *them*; but he doesn't want to talk with him at the moment. "Go help your mother set up the buffet," he says morosely.

Not long ago Lewis had an unsettling experience. He had been complaining at the Riverview about St. Dennis's aloofness—the old man had to protect his privacy, but he was being remarkably unfriendly. He declined most invitations and seemed rather uncomfortable around the department and had not—so far as Lewis knew—invited anyone to his apartment yet; one might reasonably expect an invitation for tea or sherry, certainly...? Rumor had it that he spent a fair amount of time at the local library—the *local* library, not the university's. There, in that dismal tatty place, amid the shelves of murder mysteries and women's romances and science fiction, where a single work of Flaubert's— *Madame Bovary*, of course—was nearly crowded off the shelf by Hedda Strange Fleuve's oeuvre of fifteen novels (all Gothic romances), and where a shelf called, simply, *Poetry*, was less than an arm's length and consisted of several oversized "treasuries" of "best-loved" poems and did not contain Yeats or Eliot and still less Albert St. Dennis—there, sipping tea with the aged librarian, Woodslee's Distinguished Professor of Poetry was content to chat about gardening and birdlore and the Queen and memories of England in the twenties and thirties. (The librarian, a Mrs. Willard, had been born in Manchester and had come to the United States with her husband in 1938.) Rumor had it, Lewis had complained irritably, that St. Dennis wasted hours there and even had begun to cheat on his responsibilities at the university; several students had gone to see him with their poems and had found his door locked. Of course he was a fine man, Lewis said, and possibly a genius, but...but it was disappointing, after all.

"But you people are so bourgeois," a young man had said.

Astonished, Lewis had not known how to reply. The charge was absurd, of course. But what about the librarian—? Surely she was "bourgeois." And it was a

149

ludicrous accusation to make against Lewis Seidel, of all people: hadn't the young man read *Cul-de-sac?*

He had, he believed, successfully argued the young man down, but the accusation stayed with him. It had been delivered in so casual and even rather affectionate a way....*Bourgeois. You people are so bourgeois.* Could it be possible that students thought of Lewis Seidel as merely one of a group, a faculty member like any other ...? Could it be possible that his uniqueness was not recognized, that he might be confused from a distance with such ordinary academics as Warren Hochberg and George Housley and Gowan Vaughan-Jones and old Blaise Perrin and Gladys Fetler...? (He and Gladys were the department's most popular teachers, an embarrassment to Lewis. Everyone loved Gladys, but it was widely known that her Shakespeare course was no more than a superior high school course, and that students enrolled in it cynically, being assured of fairly high grades. Whereas Lewis was demanding; he had a reputation as a difficult marker; his droll remarks often went over his students' heads.)...It seemed to him cruel and unjust.

Since that afternoon at the Riverview, however, he has come to hear, in his own words, in his characteristic phrases, a certain queer hollowness, a predictability he had never noticed before. His denunciation of modernist art—of "serious" art—his puckish anomolies and his hearty support of the near-unknown ("Nate Fulmer is the greatest living black writer"; "Geraldine McIvor is the greatest living woman poet") and his dazzling paradoxes ("The highest art is no art at all"), not to mention his outrageous judgements ("*Dracula* is the greatest novel in English literature"; "*Gone With the Wind* tells us more about the American Depression than all of Dos Passos and Farrell"), have come to sound—incredibly, horribly—*bourgeois.*

How has it happened? His rude lusty jocose defiance...his irrepressible high spirits...his marvelous sly wit and his fearlessness at making quite clear exactly where he "stands"...his tolerance of the opinions of young people and blacks and women...his continuing skirmishes with the administration and with all forms of authority...his casual but intense liaisons

150

with certain girl students (less frequent in the past few years, it must be admitted: but then he has been very busy with his writing)...his slashing reviews of others' books...his notoriously high standards...his flamboyant gestures, his sometimes coarse vocabulary, his frankly ribald anecdotes about famous people he has known...his tigerish playfulness, his unpredictability: how has it all come to seem predictable? He listens to his own voice as he lectures to his classes and he begins to tremble, perspiration breaks out on his forehead, he hears the familiarity, the staleness, the...the Seidel manner: what on earth has happened? The mirror shows a stylishly dressed man of early middle age, possibly a little heavy—no more than most of his friends, however—his face kindly with laugh lines, his pale blue eyes round and boyish with perverse innocence; he is no longer handsome, but he is still quite attractive. An expert showman, a jester. Shocking, really. Scandalous at times. At times outrageous. But—

Fifty-one years old.

Phi Beta Kappa in his junior year at City College; prizes as an undergraduate; high praise and encouragement from his professors. A Woodrow Wilson Fellowship for graduate work at Columbia. High grades, high expectations, a series of articles published in his twenties, a considerable name for himself before the age of thirty; an appointment at Brown that had not worked out; a year in England; more articles and reviews and the appointment at prestigious Woodslee; the controversial *Cul-de-sac* and more articles and reviews and.... He is often invited to give addresses at universities and women's clubs; surely that means something. And in their several conversations together he and Albert St. Dennis have seemed to strike a certain note of accord—an amiable kind of discord, it might be said; St. Dennis sees in him someone to be taken very seriously. (Even the dandyish *arriviste* Oliver Byrne takes Lewis seriously: he knows and respects Lewis's position on certain ideological and philosophical issues over which the men have differed.)

But—

In horror he glances at his watch and sees that it is 10:05.

He hurries back inside. What a commotion! Laughter, raised voices, Brad Keough playfully and drunkenly banging on a table, Gowan Vaughan-Jones shouting at Todd Andress, very nearly in tears—what on earth?—vast clouds of smoke—faces—a reeling nightmarish carnival. Trembling, he reaches for a drink someone has abandoned on the cobbler's bench. An inch or two of Scotch, a sliver of ice. He gulps it down. Coughs. Faye is searching for him—he knows that desperate glassy look of hers—*How I hate these parties*, she will scream at him tomorrow, *how I hate your awful friends!*—and he ducks into his study to escape, but there is Leslie Cullendon haranguing a subdued, frightened little group—the Swanson girl, the Jaeger girl, and Babs—wildly and happily drunk, he shouts in a voice like frayed twine something incomprehensible that sounds like *Kidney of Bloom pray for us! Kidney of Bloom pray for us! Sweets of Sin pray for us! Beer beef battledog buybull businum barnum buggerum bishop! BEER BEEF BATTLEDOG—*

His back to the rest of the party, there stands Alexis Kessler, a drink in hand, a cigarette stuck in his mouth as a child might smoke, sucking at it with great concentration. He is coolly looking through some papers and magazines lying on top of Lewis's desk; he has even moved Lewis's quartz paperweight aside. Lewis stares at him. Slowly, with that air of calm contempt that Lewis finds maddening, Alexis turns slightly and raises his eyes to Lewis's face. He says nothing. He does not blush, he is not even mildly startled or embarrassed; he merely returns Lewis's gaze. Lewis wants to rush at him, strike his absurd face, spill some blood onto his elegant clothes.... Tear a handful of hair out of his head.... He does approach Kessler, his hands shaking; in a lowered voice he says, not wishing anyone else to hear, "So you're fucking Stott, are you! So—!" and still Kessler shows no sign of emotion, he merely sucks at his cigarette and says loudly, loud enough for the others in the room to hear, "Would you prefer that I fuck you, Lewis?"

Lewis retreats.

He hurries along the corridor and pauses at the kitchen door, panting. That noise? Telephone? Doorbell? Another attack of coughing, hard to get his breath, he shuts his eyes for a moment and tries to remember... what was he doing, where was he going? Must help Faye with the food. Must go upstairs and change his clothes first: underwear soaking. Sweated through. Then out on the porch, waiting for St. Dennis, sudden chill, a mistake. Flu going around Woodslee. Sweating, shivering. Another drink would help. But if he cuts through the kitchen Faye will get him. But....

That bastard Kessler: impossible.

What had he said...?

Impossible.

Lewis wipes his face on his shoulder, catches his breath, pushes the swinging door open. A blast of heat. Charlotte Haas in one of Faye's aprons, Mona Cuffe on her way out the other door to the dining room, carrying a heavy tray. Lewis helps her; makes a show of being gallant and flirtatious. Mona giggles. Or is it Mona. The younger wives have come to resemble one another over the years. Where is Vivian? Avoided him all evening. Or has he avoided her?... He sets the tray down on the table, wipes his face again, trying to catch his breath. Brigit Stott turns from a conversation with Roger Haas and, seeing Lewis, is about to say something amusing and malicious but pauses, suddenly concerned, and asks him if he feels all right?—he's looking rather flushed—

"Is that the doorbell?" Lewis says, cupping his ear.

"The doorbell? I didn't hear anything."

There is an enormous spread of food, a holiday of food, and many of the guests are already eating. They are grouped about the table, partly blocking traffic between the rooms. Noisy cheerful merry group. Friends. Colleagues. There is Stanislaus Chung, grinning his broad "American" grin, picking at the roast beef: he seems to be inspecting it, shaking pieces off his fork that fail to meet his approval, too fatty or gristly, perhaps: he is in an unusually good mood tonight. There is Matt Ryerson, laughing heartily, showing an ex-

153

panse of gum. There is Faye, smiling her strained hostess' smile, caught in a conversation with George Housley, who is vehement about something—eroding standards at the university, perhaps—and Lewis looks quickly away, not wishing to be drawn to his wife's side. This is a party, after all; *his* party; he wants to enjoy himself....Gaylord Fraser of the drama department is standing in a corner beside a Rockwell Kent lithograph, eating hungrily. His paper plate is heaped high with food and Lewis, flinching, sees that some potato salad falls to the floor...but Gaylord doesn't appear to notice. Just then Edie Ryerson sails up to Lewis, arms opened wide as if she were going to embrace him. It is only a gesture, Lewis knows; still, it unnerves him. She asks if she may fix him a plate of this delicious food...? No. No thank you. He'll eat later. The doorbell is ringing. Has the reporter for the *Post* left yet? It's 10:15. He hopes she will excuse him but he must answer the door—there's no time to lose—

"Lewis, you don't look well at all!" Edie cries accusingly.

Lewis grimaces at her and makes his way to the foyer and there, as in a dream, he sees Oliver Byrne and St. Dennis. No: Oliver Byrne and Marilyn. Harry is helping Marilyn with her coat. Lewis staggers forward, disbelieving. "What—what is it?" he cries. "Where is he?"

Oliver Byrne looks around in amazement.

"Where is the old man? What's going on? Is he here? Where is he?"

Suddenly the babble quiets; Lewis's raised voice is a shriek.

"Do you mean—St. Dennis isn't here? You didn't bring him?"

Oliver tries to explain that St. Dennis was too tired to come to the party and is very, very sorry—he isn't a young man, after all, and the hour's reading took a great deal out of him. "He asked Marilyn and me to tell you how enormously sorry he is to miss the party in his honor," Oliver says, "how much he regrets having to go home instead—"

"Home!" Lewis cries. "What do you mean—*home?* Is

that where he is? In bed? It's only ten o'clock! What the hell is going on here, Oliver? I want to know—what the hell is going on!"

"Why, Lewis," Marilyn says in a small frightened voice, "what's wrong? You look so angry—"

Lewis ignores her. She is about to touch his sleeve and he brushes her away. "Look, Byrne," he says, "I'm asking you what's going on! What your purpose is! This party for St. Dennis has been planned for weeks—everyone has come to meet him—*everyone*—and you're not going to ruin things! Oh no! I'll drive over there and get him myself!"

"Lewis," Oliver says, "you'd better calm down. I'm not going to tolerate—"

"You're not going to tolerate! Not going to tolerate!" Lewis cries in derision. He half turns to the others, who are looking on in silence; he winks over his shoulder at Gladys Fetler, who is standing nearby, white-haired and aghast. "I know very well what your game is, Byrne—I *know*. You deliberately took the old man home, didn't you? To ruin my plans for this evening? Because you're jealous—jealous and spiteful and—and frightened—You're afraid of St. Dennis's affection for me, aren't you? You've been keeping him to yourself but it won't work—it won't work—I see through your clumsy plotting and I'm going to get him and bring him back here and—"

Afterward, versions of the struggle between Lewis and Oliver varied greatly. A number of guests claimed that Oliver tried to restrain Lewis by touching his arm and Lewis flipped Oliver's hand away and accidentally slapped him; Gladys Fetler is certain that it was an accident. ("Lewis is a good, gentle soul who wouldn't hurt anyone in the world," Gladys says.) Sandra Jaeger, however, who had hurried to the study doorway when the shouting began, claims to have seen quite clearly Lewis Seidel striking Dean Byrne in the face. How quickly it happened! How horrified she was! And then the spurt of blood, the shock of blood on Byrne's shirt front and on his handsome silk tie...! Charlotte Haas, who had come up behind Lewis from the kitchen, was amazed to see Marilyn Byrne staggering back against the umbrella stand as if shoved—but she isn't certain that Lewis really shoved her or if it simply appeared that way. Gowan Vaughan-Jones speaks of the incident in a slow, drawling, distracted manner, pushing his glasses up in order to rub at his eyes, as if he can't quite believe what he evidently saw; he hasn't been able to sleep well in the days following the scuffle. Todd Andress, over-excitable and glittery-eyed and very young, claims to have seen the Dean of Humanities poke Lewis Seidel in the chest before the shouting even began, but no one else supports him; most of the onlookers are uncertain about what really happened. They only know that something happened at the Seidels' party on Friday night in honor of Albert St. Dennis—they aren't even certain if St. Dennis was there or not. (In some versions of the story, repeated throughout the week and radiating outward from the humanities division itself, it will be claimed that the visiting English poet, St. Dennis, was the person who started a fist fight: a tough wiry little bantam of a man, and seventy-five years old! Quite a character!)

But everyone at the party heard Lewis's despairing bawl and everyone who could see him was astonished at his flushed, tear-streaked face. "You can't do this to me!" he cried. "You can't—any of you! I've waited so long and you can't—I won't let you! *I won't let you!*"

A few minutes before midnight Alexis lies in Brigit Stott's bed, stroking the cat nestled against his side, her head on his stomach, golden floating lovely notes in his mind, a melody so exquisite he cannot quite believe in it: he plays and replays it, slows it, expands it, embellishes it. One of his songs for St. Dennis. His. The third song of the cycle.

It has come to him, nearly complete, in the last twenty minutes.

Brigit is in the bathroom showering, to get the odor of smoke out of her hair; Alexis is too lazy to bother; Alexis is sleepy and drunk and quite content, rubbing the cat's ears and beneath her chin. The melody plays itself effortlessly. Ah: like that. Yes. Alexis's toes twitch with the rhythm of the piece. Languid and lovely. Music. Melody. A song for soprano voice, accompanied by piano. Very simple, almost ascetic. The sorrow of St. Dennis's words, austere, tragic, no self-pity. How love flares up in the blood like an infection, raging, carrying all before it...how one's blood is overheated, the brain disturbed...how it must necessarily pass ...must rise and fall and fade...like a principle of nature over which human wishes have no power. ...Alexis lies with his eyes open, seeing nothing. The cat stretches out beside him. In the bathroom the shower door opens and closes, Brigit calls out to him, Alexis pretends not to hear, listening to the melody in his imagination. Yes: like that. And then slowing. (But must be careful, since the melody is starting to drift into something by Fauré, the main theme of one of Fauré's piano quartets.)

Alexis does not think of the party at the Seidels': those frantic noisy pathetic people. The ravaged young man in the wheelchair eating huge slices of baked ham, mustard falling onto his wasted shanks; the girl in the metallic silver outfit complaining in a small, pretty, frightened voice that the university had gone back on its word about something—some part-time job for her; Lewis Seidel red-faced and shouting, a maniac, a fool, having to be restrained by his own son. These images flit through Alexis's mind but he does not really think of them....And there is Brigit herself, Brigit of whom he is very fond, sobbing into his shoulder as soon as they were alone; as upset by the incident as if Lewis had attacked her and not Byrne, or as if Lewis were her husband and therefore her responsibility. Why so upset? Why so distraught? He had tried to joke with her. Her breath reeked of gin. Her make-up was smeared. (Before St. Dennis's reading Alexis and Brigit had showered together, here in Brigit's apartment. They had been playful as young animals, kissing and hugging and soaping each other; Alexis had shampooed her hair, digging his fingers into her scalp. Then, afterward, he had dried her in a large bath towel and wrapped another towel about her hair and, despite her protests, he had examined her face closely...had rubbed cold cream into her skin...had taken a tweezers and plucked at her eyebrows to make their arch more prominent, raised high above the eye...all the while half-scolding her for not cultivating her appearance more assiduously: didn't she know her facial bones were marvelous, her eyes marvelous, she was a woman of beauty who must take responsibility for herself? Brigit was embarrassed, Brigit wanted to escape. Always so self-conscious! He teased her, kissed her, made her stand obediently still as he worked on her face. There is nothing pretty about you, he said, nothing conventionally pretty. You're either beautiful or ugly. I don't mind you ugly—it's a severe, intelligent ugliness. Stand still! Stop blushing!...But you can be beautiful too, for a while at least; with those cheekbones you can be beautiful for another fifteen or twenty years. You're enviable, in fact. I wouldn't mind being you....Why are you so self-conscious, Brigit? Do you imagine that your face and your body are your own, your private possessions? Not any longer!

(He had rubbed more cream into her face, and oily lotion onto her body—her small, slightly sagging breasts, her stomach, her hips and buttocks and thighs and legs, even her feet, her small perfect toes that he couldn't help kissing; he had insisted upon cutting her toenails and filing her fingernails and polishing them —he discovered, in her medicine cabinet, an old but still usable bottle of nail polish in a quite attractive shade—opalescent pink-pearl; he put her make-up on for her, stroking the skin of her face upward, gently, while she stood, flushed and subdued, her eyes half-closed as if they had just made love and there was no spirit in her to protest or even to respond any longer. The flesh-colored make-up, faint smears of rouge on her cheekbones very lightly rubbed in, very lightly and subtly, and eye shadow, and eye liner, and inky-black mascara, and her eyebrows penciled in lightly, and lipstick...and he had seen, enchanted, a woman's beautiful image emerge from the plain and rather sallow material he had been given: ah, how he loved her! How mesmerizing she was!)

Digging his fingers into the cat's fur, hearing again the melody and moving with it, seeming to rise with it...he is pleasantly drowsy, his body satiated, at rest. The party is nearly forgotten; it has no meaning to him. (Brigit, talking to him from the bathroom, is evidently still upset. She uses expressions like "worried," "concerned," "frightened." Alexis mumbles a reply.) A few faces rise again and pop like bubbles: the hard, handsome woman with the mole on her upper lip, the Italian girl with the lovely bright dark eyes, the boy in the denim outfit with the shy, awkward smile—Seidel's son—approaching Alexis in the study to ask if he, Alexis, is the musician, the composer. But the faces disappear, the party itself whirls and vanishes. What does any of it matter to Alexis? He sees again St. Dennis on the stage, behind the podium; a lonely figure. ("Your name is—Alexander?" "Alexis. Alexis Kessler." "Oh— my dear, yes! Yes. I remember now—we corresponded, didn't we? You sent me that charming picture of yourself.")

The song of St. Dennis shapes itself in Alexis's mind, the loveliest melody he has ever written. He *knows* it is good.

He sits up suddenly. He is fully awake now; a thought has just penetrated his reverie. Brigit's longhaired black cat Minnie gazes at him attentively. Her eyes are yellow. Her small pink tongue protrudes slightly beneath her black nose. She is very fond of her mistress' young lover, she likes nothing better than to nudge and nuzzle him, and purr her hoarse crackling purr, and get him to dig his nails in her hide. But Alexis hardly notices her now. He is thinking that he must get away: must get away to work, to write those notes down, to labor until they are perfect.

Brigit, just leaving the bathroom, is speaking of an odd conversation she had with Roger Haas, the university's chief counsel; denuded of make-up she looks sallow, tired, wan, her severely plucked eyebrows are almost invisible, her expression strikes Alexis as querulous. Had he heard, she says, that someone in political science was actually being sued by one of the big paperpulp companies downriver because he had said in a lecture that the Powhatan was being polluted by local industry—

"Brigit," Alexis says, "can I borrow five hundred dollars? I'm leaving Woodslee for a few days—for a week. I need to work without interruption."

Brigit stares at him as if uncomprehending. Her robe had come partway open, and now she draws it shut, staring.

"Five hundred dollars," Alexis says, somewhat impatiently. "Could you write me a check before we go to bed? Or do you have cash?"

At Albert St. Dennis's
and
At the Housleys'

December 31, 7 p.m.

"I can't go there. I can't talk to those wretched people."

"Come on, Sandra, for Christ's sake—"

"I can't."

She is lying in bed, cringing beneath the blanket. The wall is two or three inches from her face; she appears to be staring at it. Much time has passed. Hours. Days. Someone has switched on the overhead light, which they rarely use because it is too bright, too glaring, and now he stands over her, and now he is tugging at the blanket. He wants to pull it away from her, wants to expose her. She is shivering violently.

"Sandra, for Christ's sake, please—You've got to help me—"

She can hear his breathing.

Panting.

In despair, in befuddlement. She stares at the wall but it has no surface—there are no cracks, no patterns, nothing to catch the eye. She might be looking into a depthless substance. Where does it end, where are its limits? Her shoulders are hunched and her arms are tightly crossed. Her bare feet are very cold—her toes hurt with the cold. When she went to bed the other day their thermometer out back read –15°F.

"Sandra, are you sick? Is there really something wrong? Should I—Would you like—Is there anything I can do?"

Her teeth have begun chattering.

Ernest stands over the bed, tall and baffled and outraged. His voice is not familiar. She hears the disgust in it: his astonishment at her failure. Unwashed hair, unwashed body, sleep-encrusted eyes.

"Should I call a doctor...?" he says faintly.

He has spoken of calling a doctor before, when she first went to bed—the last week of November, when the news came; and again a few days ago, when they returned from a three-day visit with Sandra's family in Springfield, Massachusetts. Unwashed, hair in greasy strands, face swollen, eyes puffy. His lovely wife.

But he will not call a doctor, she knows.

"Honey, let me help you up. All right? Honey?...I could help you take a bath and you could wear that long dress and we wouldn't need to stay at the party very long; we could stay an hour or so, that wouldn't be too much for you, would it...? Sandra? We've already missed the Hochbergs' open house and Dr. Fetler's ...and.... Why don't you wear that silver outfit, honey, maybe that would be more comfortable.... Do you hear me, Sandra? Honey?"

He pulls the blanket away from her shoulders. She tries to clutch at it but her fingers are too cold; it slips away.

She begins to cry.

She cannot remember who he is. A young husband. Her husband. She has not eaten for nearly two days. The bed seems to be tilting, lurching. What if she falls...? But she is safe, someone is holding her, his face buried against her neck and hair. One arm tight around her. The bed trembling with his sobs.

"Oh Jesus I'm so sorry, what can I do, I'm so sorry, so sorry," he cries. "What can I do...? There's nothing I can do."

He lies beside her, hugging her. He is very warm, very agitated. She brings his hand to her face, kisses it, presses it against her cheek....it seems to her that time winks and yawns suddenly, that the two of them slide into an abyss, into the depthless wall, no weight to them; they might plunge like this, in each other's arms, helpless, forever. He sobs that he loves her. He doesn't know what to do—what else to do. This vacation has been hellish because they've had too much time to think, too much time to worry, going over and over

163

again the possibilities—hearing each other say the same things again and again—confined here in this tiny apartment where they have no choice except to talk about it, and then at her parents' where they could not even allude to it but had to tell so many lies: he knows it's been hell for her. But in a week the new semester will begin. Maybe things will change. It may be they are exaggerating it all...that they will look back on this in a few years and find it all amusing.

She hears the anguish in his voice. She lies with his warm hand pressed against her face, wanting suddenly to laugh; something convulses in her throat and she has to hold herself still. Amusing. Amusing! Why not reinterpret this hell as amusing, once they are out of it? She has already spoken philosophically and with an admirable degree of control, some days ago, when the first of Ernest's letters of application to other universities were answered, when the first of the form letters arrived, that her feelings were probably exaggerated because of the time of year; she was not really depressed, not seriously depressed; of course she would get better. Isn't there something about December...the completion of a cycle...a sense of life at its weakest, as the sun is at its weakest, a dull glowering white ...dusk in the afternoon, the mornings a perpetual twilight...the universe filling up with snow.... It has nothing to do with their situation, does it, the dreary freezing weather and the gravitational pull toward darkness, toward death, doesn't everyone feel it, the pulse of life growing fainter and fainter until it seems so easy to let go...?

In a few minutes his sobs stop. He is really all right; he is not going to break down. Sandra lies in his arms, feeling the curious weightlessness of their marriage. There is no substance to them, she might drift from his embrace or he from hers, slipping free, boundless. Their embraces are desperate and their tears are genuine. Their love for each other is genuine. But it has no power to save them: it is this understanding that has terrified her.

In Cambridge several years ago they had gone to a film festival and saw for the first time a film by Truffaut called *Shoot the Piano Player*, which they had liked very much. They had held hands in the crowded theater, had kissed, had poked at each other when something on screen especially delighted them. Back in September, however, they had seen the film again when it was shown at the university, along with a number of other Truffaut films, and the very first sequence —the first two or three minutes—had struck them both as transparent and banal and flat; to their astonished disappointment the film, as it moved along, was not the same film they had admired, but another, lesser, quite unconvincing work that had lost its magic. Sandra had not wanted to speak of her disappointment to Ernest, but midway through the film he asked if they should leave?—and she got to her feet at once.

For some time afterward they discussed that perplexing experience. Had it been the film itself that failed, or had they failed; had they somehow lost the emotional key to a work of art...? Or was it possible they mourned not simply their inability to relive an experience but, in a profoundly disturbing way, their realization that the original experience had been spurious...?

Magic might depart from every experience: this was the possibility that terrified.

On this freezing, windy, attentuated day, the final day of the year, Brigit Stott prepares herself for a New Year's Eve party and thinks of mortality.

She has been thinking of mortality for some time. The past two weeks, the past several months, the past five years. Mortality, mutability, death, she thinks; what other thoughts are worthy of our attention?—and yet, what other thoughts evoke in us such a sense of luxurious futility?

She is in love and therefore thinks of death: it is a romantic reaction, an instinctive impulse. Wishing to live and wishing to live keenly in the body—as she has not lived for years—she naturally thinks of the body's breakdown, its perverse but inevitable failure. But she is unable to imagine herself aged. There are models and images of age for her—two grandmothers, a grandfather; even St. Dennis; even, at times, at the very end of a school day, Gladys Fetler herself. But Brigit is unable to think of herself in these terms. For several years death wore her husband's face—came to her in dreams and in waking visions with that man's strangely commonplace appearance, his look of being quite ordinary. Though she lived with Stanley Fifield for more than a decade she isn't altogether certain of what he looks like, and she suspects that she, to him, is a ghostly, maddening presence. Having been so close, so compulsively intimate, how could they have failed to be blinded to each other...? If it did not hurt so much, if the abrasions were not, still, so embarrassingly raw, Brigit would write about her marriage: but she hasn't the courage. She hasn't the distance. Throughout the marriage she was cursed by a sense of his not knowing her and not wishing to know her; not *her*. He fell in love with and married a certain young woman, an image in his imagination, and he did not want this image violated. He fought for it passionately and viciously, as if it were life itself—he fought Brigit for it, in fact. Making love with him in the customary dark she had often thought, though every instinct in her tried to forbid the thought, that she was, at such times, only a physical stimulus for him—a means of stirring his manly desire, his "love"— which thrust itself desperately and wildly and ecstatically into a ghostly image of Brigit Stott, a vapor that had no relationship to the living woman at all. And when she could not respond to his love he had been murderously resentful—as he would naturally be, as any man naturally would be; in a way she could not blame him. She had thought—is all love founded upon such illusions?—is pleasure in the flesh, like the pleasure of art, possible only when the imagination wills the outer world into the form it desires? If this were true it was not a cynical truth, only a truth that must be faced. But she did not really believe it. She could not believe it. My experience is unique, she thought, it doesn't touch upon anyone else's, the world would have collapsed centuries ago if my experience were everyone's....She believed in love, still; she believed in others' beliefs in love. A single failed marriage does not call into question all marriages. A single disappointing husband is not a judgment upon all men. And it worries her that she alone of all Stanley's acquaintances is the one least able to know him. She could describe him only with difficulty—the outward, physical appearance of the man, his deliberate cultivation of certain styles of dress and hair and mannerisms that identified him with the smartly affluent, even the vocabulary he affected, even his tone of voice, at times, seemed strategies of disguise rather than expressions of his unique personality. The public self, the private self, the husband and the lover and the man and the human being with his own raw, indescribable need were all different, always at war. She had been a minor casualty of that war.

But it is Alexis she thinks of, not Stanley; she has not seen Stanley for over a year, and apart from random reports on his behavior from friends (most recently, just before Christmas: a woman friend living in New York telephoned Brigit to talk of various things and brought up, as if incidentally, the subject of Brigit's husband and his continued abuse of her—less slanderous now than in the past but still imaginative and distressing), she knows nothing of his life. She wants to know nothing; she would like to forget. Alexis dominates her thoughts, and if she finds herself thinking of death, of extinction, it slips about her with an air of being, somehow, related to her lover....She wants to live, she wants to live passionately. But it seems to her that it is only through Alexis that she can live; almost, in a way, it is only through his embrace, his awakening of passion in her. She sees through him, through his vision. She hears through him. The life in her arteries and nerves and marrow seems no longer her own but his. He has, therefore, without wanting it, the power of death over her....At the same time she rejects this as grotesquely romantic. She does not believe it at all.

(When her friend telephoned two weeks ago Alexis was with her; it was after dinner and the two of them had been cleaning up the kitchen. Brigit made the mistake of accepting the call, of talking animatedly within Alexis's earshot, and she must have mentioned Stanley's name, because after a few minutes Alexis came to her and took the receiver from her and put it quietly back down. She had been amazed and rather angry, and he had been calm at first and then angry and then furious and then hysterical: they had ended up screaming at each other. He did not want her to talk to others while he was with her—he did not want her to *care* enough about her husband to even inquire about him. Didn't she know, he raged, what an insult that was to him? Was she so insensitive she didn't understand—?)

That Brigit Stott could imagine her life dependent upon anyone else, especially upon *him*: it is absurd, really. A grotesque exaggeration.

It is only 7:10. She has been awake since six that

morning, thinking about Alexis, about the party tonight, about the direction in which her life seems to be
plunging. She can barely recall the days before she met
him, back in September; it seems to her, now, that those
days were a preparation for their meeting. She cannot
imagine this winter without him. She cannot even
imagine this party tonight—at St. Dennis's—without
him. Last Christmas she made the egregious error of
accepting her mother's invitation to visit with them
and had returned to Woodslee only two days after
Christmas, almost suicidal. Apart from a hectic, totally
unpremeditated hour in an ice-cream shop with her
sister Janet and her sister's two young children, during
which Brigit flinched at the little girls' excitement but
enjoyed it all the same—enjoyed being an aunt, enjoyed
feeding a one-year-old ice cream in an atmosphere of
simulated wrought-iron tables and chairs and pepper-
mint-stick walls, and rediscovered her genuine liking
for her sister despite their great differences; and apart
from the first night's blissful dreamless sleep (she had
driven down from Woodslee alone, non-stop), she had
found the experience torturous, and had wondered seriously whether she could ever bring herself to visit
Norfolk again. It was not simply her parents' and her
relatives' smugness, their complacency in terms of their
own lives, and not even their disapproval of her hus-
bandless state; and not even—though this hurt—their
indifference to her writing and her university teaching;
it was their air of resentment—her father's almost rude
rejection of her offer to help her mother and him financially. (Mr. Stott was partly retired from his real-
estate business in a Norfolk suburb, having had a mild
heart attack the year before. He had been, in his prime,
"underfoot" in local politics, though he had never run
for public office and had never aspired—had never
dared aspire, relatives said behind his back—to anything more than a mayor's aide or a committee chairman for the county. Having complained about money
all the years that Brigit lived at home, he had evidently
stopped talking or thinking about it at all, perhaps out
of shame or dread; at any rate Brigit had annoyed him
on Christmas Day, of all times, bringing up the subject

of money in the bright gay-girlish manner she had cultivated years ago, which had charmed him once. A terrible mistake: he had been sullen the rest of the day.... Alone in her old room she had wept with frustration and dismay. How unfair he was, how ridiculous her parents were! All of them! Herself included! There was to be no overt quarrel between them but she left ahead of schedule just the same, and it seemed to her that no one had seriously tried to prevent her leaving.)

The Christmas before, she had become involved, against her saner judgment, with a Woodslee student, a girl of nineteen with apparently insurmountable problems—a lover, parents in the process of getting divorced, other professors who did not understand her. The girl had been pretty enough, and lively, and intelligent, but there was something alarmingly infantile about her, and once Brigit befriended her—after a stormy, tearful session in her office at the university—the girl became quite dependent upon her. She brought Brigit pages from her journal, talked to Brigit at great length about her apocalyptic dream-visions, her tumultuous love affair with a young man studying forestry at a nearby state university, her parents' hatred for each other and their paranoid suspicions about her, her problems with drugs, alcohol, common aspirin, and Coke. Having received a grade of D− at mid-term from Brigit, she wisely withdrew from Brigit's course in the American novel, but she kept coming to Brigit's office, sometimes twice a day, and was so weak, so troubled, so tearful that Brigit could not turn her aside. Just before Christmas the girl had a crisis of some sort—a "spiritual crisis," she called it— and was afraid she would kill herself if she remained in the girls' residence hall, so she came to Brigit's apartment and was allowed to move in temporarily.... Two years later the episode strikes Brigit as merely ludicrous; she cannot believe she was ever so naive. How had it happened, Brigit Stott manipulated so blandly! Brigit, who prided herself on her cynicism! The girl, whose name was Kim, and whose outfit was a single filthy pair of blue jeans and one or two filthy cashmere sweaters, simply moved in with Brigit and stayed for eighteen days. She

170

smoked, she drank can after can of Coke, she walked about barefoot, she crooned to the cat and slept on Brigit's sofa, nude beneath a blanket, and snored so loudly that Brigit had trouble sleeping; she chattered to Brigit or to herself, she was constantly singing under her breath, she pleaded with Brigit to allow her to "help" with her novel—she could type, maybe, or she could provide descriptions or dialogue; surely there was something she could do, her high-school English teachers had praised her "gift for expressing herself" so highly—? Brigit spent more and more time at her office in the Humanities Building or in the university library or walking aimlessly about the campus, homeless herself, spiteful and outwitted, and though she rehearsed innumerable speeches she was never able, to her shame, to ask the girl to leave. It happened, simply, that the girl left. One afternoon. Brigit returned from the library to find a note on the coffee table: *Dear B., Hate to run out on you like this just before Christmas without even a personal good-by & thanks but I got a chance for a ride all the way to Ft. Lauderdale & he's leaving right now. Thanx a Million for Everything. Love, Kim.*

The girl left Woodslee, and as far as Brigit was able to discover, she never returned. The first week of January Brigit received her telephone bill and was astonished to see that the girl had run up a bill of $240—telephone calls to Los Angeles; to Madison, Wisconsin; to Baton Rouge, Louisiana; to New York City. There was something frightening about the experience, Brigit thought afterward: not just the girl's placid assumption that she would be cared for, not even her selfishness, but some answering assumption in Brigit herself, that she must allow this victimization, she *must* subject herself to an imposition without charm or nobility. She had known beforehand she would be disgusted with herself afterward and yet, even before the girl had pleaded with her to allow her to stay—"for a few days"—she had more or less acquiesced. It was as if she were too timid to be as cruel as her good sense directed her to be; as if she were acting out someone else's idea of Brigit Stott. But the Christmas holidays had been less burdensome than usual because she had, at least, the fuel of her anger to keep her warm. She had gone to parties, to dinners and open houses and receptions, and to a particularly noisy and drunken New Year's Eve party at the home of a sociology professor no longer at Woodslee, and, in those interstices of social occasions that are so painful because one feels, at such times, doubly alone, she had at least the image of Kim before her—the dread of knowing she would be waiting for her at the apartment, the horror of a halfway serious belief that the girl would never leave, that she was really a daughter of Brigit's and her responsibility forever.

(When a Woodslee student committed suicide last March by taking an overdose of barbiturates, Brigit heard the news with unreasonable horror—she had the idea that the girl must somehow be Kim and that she, Brigit, was guilty of not having prevented the suicide. It turned out she did not know the girl at all; but her first reaction had been one of panic.)

Sixteen years ago....

She does not wish to think of suicide; not tonight.

She switches on the light above her narrow balcony and stands close against the cold windowpane, staring out. That hardcrusted look of intense cold: must be at least ten degrees below zero. A certain cruel, gritty radiance to the snow. Beautiful. The light shows uneven dunes of a few inches on the balcony floor and on the narrow railing. A thin scattering of seed for the wild birds, now partly covered by snow. (Earlier that day a number of hungry birds descended upon Brigit's balcony and she rejoiced in their fluttering busyness and the surprise of their color: several cardinals, two mourning doves, house sparrows and slate-colored juncos and a single chickadee, and the jay with its broken and now withered left leg, all picking in the seed. That they were oblivious of her and cared nothing for her admiration made the experience all the more valuable: they descended like grace, unbidden, unearned, impermanent, quite beyond her control.) Past the railing there is a formless dark penumbra. Lightly falling snowflakes, again and always, a day and an evening
172

and a night filling up with snow, a harsh wind from the northeast, from Lake Champlain, from the future. The temperature has not risen much above zero for the past week. Each year this long holiday period seems to Brigit more mysteriously depressing. Perhaps it is her age—she will be thirty-nine next August—and she has lived through the cycle too many times. Yet there is always something jarring about the power of this time of year to affect her: a familiarity that carries within it a sense of profound mystery. Even when the sun glares in a blankly blue sky and the heaped-up banks of snow are surpassingly beautiful there is something tenuous about the world and about her position in it. A physical organism, of course, a distinct physical entity with sense enough to preserve her being, and even to persevere—but drawn to what is not human, what is defiantly not human, in the glacial landscape and in the pale-glowing winter sun. She yearns for something, she yearns to surrender to something, that almost tactile gravitational pull toward dark and quiet and sleep and death....

Only 7:25. The party Albert St. Dennis is giving doesn't begin until 9:00; and it isn't clear whether Alexis will stop by for her—he is going to another party earlier in the evening, given by someone in the drama department. (He doesn't care to see these people, he claims; they bore him. But they've invited him to their home several times and he has always declined and it would be fairly easy for him to spend an hour in their company and then leave for a more important, smaller party.... He doesn't want to antagonize them, he says; he has so many enemies at Woodslee already.) Brigit was invited out to the Housleys' and she halfway regrets now that she declined the invitation, since it would give her something to do, a way of filling up time before she walks over to St. Dennis's apartment building. It might be best simply to walk, rather than call a cab or wait for Alexis; the walk is only a half mile and she has been unpleasantly inactive since classes stopped on the fifteenth of December. A few discouraging days spent on her work: looking through graduate students' term papers, rereading *The Wings of the*

Dove, writing a page and a half on her novel and discarding it and returning again to her students' papers; several social events—a dinner at the Haases'; a small luncheon given by an unusually agitated and verbose Marilyn Byrne for women faculty members; a pointlessly huge open house at the Garretts' which she and Alexis attended together, and left together after forty-five minutes; Gladys Fetler's usual punch party for members of the English department and favored students; and there had been something else, hadn't there, at least one other party...? Yes: an awkward buffet dinner at the Cuffes'. (Joe Cuffe is an assistant professor no longer precisely young and promising, and Brigit has heard—by way of Lewis Seidel, who perhaps should not have told her, since the information is confidential—that the man is not only not going to be promoted this year but is, very likely, going to receive notice of termination of contract; there have been rumors, more than usually hearty, about budget cuts imposed upon the departments from above, from beyond even Dean Byrne's office. Brigit knows her own position to be quite secure but nevertheless she feels a thrill of apprehension. That faintly smiling, guarded look about the Cuffes—poor Mona Cuffe's attempt at talking warmly and sincerely and intelligently with the Hochbergs—and Joe drinking too much and stumbling over Gowan Vaughan-Jones's feet: Brigit noted it all, could not help but observe, and felt the evening to be enormously depressing.)

"Stay home, then," Alexis said. "Why don't you work on your novel...? I work, don't I? I work all the time. I destroy most of what I do but at least I do it; there's some pleasure in that. Then I go out, I've earned the privilege of going out.... But you're always going out and always complaining; why don't you stay home?"

Brigit had been irritated by his tone. It was not true that she was always going out, still less that she was always complaining. She liked the Woodslee people quite a bit—she was really fond of them—quite dependent upon them. Her discontent was with herself and she thought it cruel and insensitive of her lover to attack her.

"You don't understand me," she said angrily. "...You don't love me."

Now it is 7:30. She realizes she is waiting for Alexis to call; she has been waiting most of the day.

"Bastard," she whispers.

She remembers their first meeting: the boy's filthy hands. The shock of his handsome face, the shock of his too-blond hair. When she brought up the subject of their first meeting and told him of their exchange—"If you think my hands are dirty, you should see the rest of my body"—he claimed she was mistaken: he had never said those words to her. Never. He laughed at the fact of his possibly dirty hands but did not acknowledge that either; he denied everything. "You must be confusing me with someone else," he said. He stretched his fingers wide to show her that he wasn't dirty now, he had washed his hands thoroughly before coming to her.

"I remember it very well," Brigit said stiffly.

"No, you're mistaken: mixing me up with another man."

Impossible, she thinks, to mix him up with another man.

She pours herself a drink, brings it to the balcony window, sips at it while staring at the snowflakes. This evening is far better than last New Year's Eve—incomparably better. She will be with Alexis in a short while, they will probably drink too much and stay too late, and come back here together; last New Year's she was totally alone. She had thought of suicide then, not as a possibility but as a privilege she had not earned—scoffing at herself, talking aloud, her interior harangue surfacing crazily as if, at this dull dark time of the year, the least flattering of one's thoughts demanded utterance. Suicide was not for her anyway: it wasn't imaginative enough. Those of her friends and acquaintances who had committed suicide struck Brigit as having miscalculated the significance of their lives; had they been less fascinated with themselves they might be living still. And suicide seemed to be, now, an option for younger and younger people. There were children as young as ten or eleven, she had read recently, who killed themselves, given the idea by television, perhaps, or by the example of others; the son of a casual friend of Brigit's from the early days of her marriage, certainly no more than thirteen years old, had shot himself in the base of the skull with his father's police service revolver, kept in a desk drawer in his parents' suburban home in Connecticut—Brigit had heard the news only a few weeks ago and had yet to contact her friend, couldn't think what to write, put off not only doing it but thinking about it: there seemed really nothing to say. But such acts of self-destruction could not be considered, by even the most sympathetic survivor, to be intelligent strategies. It occurred to Brigit that in her life span she had witnessed the decline of suicide as a possibility for intelligent people. What was so commonplace was obviously déclassé.

7:45. Her glass is empty.

A pity she hadn't accepted the Housleys' invitation. She is ready to leave, ready to escape this small apartment where in another few minutes she will find herself thinking of the early days of her marriage, sixteen years ago; a forbidden topic. Drinking alone is an embarrassing habit. It gives her no joy, no sense of release. Instead, it seems to loosen her control over herself, so that what has been skillfully suppressed now works its way free and rises into her consciousness. The Housleys' party was to begin at 7:30. One of their large indiscriminate gatherings, probably, at which anyone was likely to appear—Republican congressmen and their wives; elderly bachelors engaged in translations of Juvenal or Catullus, and contemptuous of all existing translations; a couple whose son might have just received a Nobel Prize in biology; administrators whom one never thought of—the Dean of Women, the registrar, the director of food service, the Assistant Dean of Commerce and Finance. Brigit had met at the Housleys' once an old gentleman whose exhaustive study of Melville she had always considered a masterpiece of scholarship and tender, fastidious criticism—the sort of work she had, in a way, once wanted to do, believing it to be less disturbing than original work and possibly more valuable. She had met the New Hampshire poet Howard Flynn at the Housleys' three years ago and
176

had almost—though not quite—made the mistake of bringing him back to her apartment with her (she learned afterward from her friend Natalie Trevor, who lived in Manhattan, of the extraordinary sexual demands Flynn commonly made—and of how disappointing he himself was as a lover); she had met a fascinating woman, a dancer, a non-resident of Woodslee, who was trying to free herself of a husband as bitter and jealous and unreasonable as Brigit's husband was being at that time, and the two talked together for hours in a corner of the Housleys' big living room—in rather strident drunken hilarious voices, Brigit supposed afterward. But there would be, mixed in with fascinating strangers, the usual people—the Hochbergs, the Seidels, Gowan Vaughan-Jones, Gladys Fetler, Perrin Blaise, possibly even Leslie Cullendon. And the Housleys lived too far away—southeast of the university, out on the Valley Mills Drive, halfway to Kittyboro. Too far to go alone.

She pours another drink.

Sixteen years ago tonight she and Stanley Fifield had been married two days. They had set out on their honeymoon, driving down the coast from New York City to Florida; they had been, at the start, quite happy. She is certain they were happy—must have been happy. A young woman of twenty-two, a young man of twenty-eight. They were in love and newly married and consequently happy. On the second-last day of their drive, however, they stayed on the highway too long; Stanley wanted to spend the night across the Florida border. Brigit drove for an hour and a half at a stretch and then Stanley took over and drove for as many as four hours in a row, just above the speed limit. He was reluctant to stop even for gas. In the Jacksonville-St. Augustine area Brigit began to feel nauseated; there was a wet, gassy, sickening stench to the air. She had never been in Florida before and it seemed rather disappointing, not much different from northern New Jersey. Stanley kept them on the road well past sunset, however, and well into the evening. (His paternal grandparents, who were fairly wealthy, owned a house in Palm Beach and it was there Brigit and Stanley were headed; the house was to be lovely—white stucco with its own beach on the ocean—and their two-week vacation was to be conventionally idyllic, though by then the marriage was more or less broken.)

They could not stop in the St. Augustine area because of the odor. Stanley did not comment on it, and Brigit dared not say very much (she sensed that her young husband felt a certain defensiveness about Florida). So he continued driving south on the interstate highway, past Crescent Beach, past Summer Haven, past Marineland and Flagler Beach and Ormond-by-the-Sea; his destination was Daytona Beach. The gassy odor gave way to freer air. It was drizzling, however, and quite dark by the time they reached Daytona Beach—Brigit estimated they had been on the road nearly ten hours.

And then Stanley began to act oddly. He passed motel after motel, slowing a little, then speeding up, always finding something wrong. Brigit was leaning forward in the passenger seat, peering through the rain at the indistinct neon signs. *Vacancy. No Vacancy.* Her vision trembled, she felt nauseated and chilled. She was so exhausted she could not trust her judgment. When Stanley slowed she stared hard at the upcoming motel, trying desperately to see if it had a vacancy, or if its rates were listed; Stanley would say, "This one? Here? How does it look?" and when she didn't reply at once he pressed down on the accelerator and drove by. She began to stammer. She looked from one side of the highway to the other. Motel after motel, neon signs, drizzle, windshield wipers, her husband's peculiar impatience, her own exhaustion. It seemed to her that they had been driving for days. The two of them, like this, driving for days without end. Stanley at the wheel, subtly angry, Brigit beside him staring ahead at the wet highway and trying to think what was going wrong. Motels, trailer courts, neon signs of pink and scarlet and blue and gold and green, the thumping of the windshield wipers, the blinding rain. "What about this one? No, on the other side, Brigit—for Christ's sake—can't you help me? It's hard enough to drive in this fucking weather—can't you at least help me with

178

the signs?" *Vacancies. No Vacancies. Closed. Open. Special Rates. No Vacancies.* There were high-rise hotels alternating with old one-story stucco motels and cottages. There were wild stretches of vacant land. On the shoulder of the highway, in the rain, stood two young people—a boy and a girl, Brigit believed—hitchhiking without much hope. Stanley sped by them at fifty miles an hour.

When Brigit pointed out a possible motel Stanley seemed not to notice it in time. Or, noticing it, he rejected it at once—it was too old-looking; it was probably too expensive. Brigit's eyes filled with tears. She was tired, so tired, she had come so far from home, she had put her trust in a young man whom she had seen, mainly, in the company of other people, at parties and in restaurants. He had been sweet and charming and witty and she had fallen in love with him, and she had married him, and now it was too late: they were searching for a motel in Daytona Beach on New Year's Eve, it was very dark, it was raining and cold and ugly. She was not Brigit Stott any longer; she was Mrs. Stanley Fiefield. She blinked at the neon signs and tried to read off their names and rates but she was never quick enough, and if Stanley did slow down it was Brigit who hesitated, certain there would be something wrong with the motel they were approaching. Stanley chuckled once or twice but did not explain himself. Sand 'n' Surf...Daytona Motel...Mayan Inn... Pirates' Cove... Red Carpet Inn...Sunshine Motor Inn...Boardwalk Inn...Surfrider Motel...Top o' the Surf...Atlantic Inn...Whispering Waves... Treasure Island...Holiday Shores Inn...Hawaiian Motel...Inlet Motor Inn ...Harbor Motor Hotel...Gull Inn...Pelican Motor Lodge...Day's End Court...Stanley drove through Daytona Beach, past the city limits, and made an abrupt, reckless U-turn on the highway, and headed back again. It was now 8:30. The rain whipped across the pavement. Brigit began to cry softly, so that her husband wouldn't hear. Again the motels, the trembling neon signs, again, again, Day's End Court...Pelican Motor Lodge...Gull Inn...Harbor Motor Hotel...."Here. This one. This is it," Stanley said suddenly, turning into one of the high-rise motels. "Goddamn it, we're not going any farther tonight."

He jumped out of the car without closing the door and hurried to the office and reappeared a minute later with the keys to a room. The two walked through the rain to an elevator and went up, silent and reeling with exhaustion, to a room on the sixth floor that overlooked the ocean, and Brigit stood there, at the window, staring stupidly out into the night, trying to determine what she must say or do. Stanley checked the bathroom, the closet, the bureau drawers. One of the lamps didn't work. The rug was stained. He asked her what she thought—was the room adequate? She said the view would probably be quite lovely in the morning. It amazed her, and rather intimidated her, that the ocean was almost directly below their back window; she opened the door to the balcony but the wind was strong, rain was coming in, she thought it wiser to close the door again. The sea air was marvelous. It was so fresh she felt dizzy. She thought—What did she think, he asked, was it adequate?—or too shabby? The stucco walls were dirty. The rug was dirty. Look at the bed-spreads—look at the cigarette burns! Or was it all right? "I don't know," Brigit said numbly. "I think...I think it's all right."

"Fine," Stanley said. "Because I can't drive any farther. Not tonight."

"The view should be—"

"I'm not going out in that car again tonight," he said.

He paced about the room, opening the bathroom door, checking the closet again, switching on the television set. He opened the door to the balcony but the ocean wind was too strong.

Brigit hugged herself, shuddering.

He looked at her.

He was young and fierce and handsome. His hair, damp from the rain, fell slanted across his forehead; his lips worked silently. She had never seen him before. She did not know him. His complexion had gone pale with exhaustion, his eyes were bloodshot.

"What's wrong?" he asked. "...You don't like the room, do you?"

"Yes," Brigit said. "It's all right."

"But you don't *like* it. You're disappointed."

"I don't know, Stanley. Please. It seems to be—"

"You aren't very enthusiastic."

"I'm tired—"

"*I'm* tired! I've been driving that fucking car for the past four hours!"

"The room is fine," Brigit said hollowly. "Why don't you check in at the office and I can bring some of the things up and—"

"You want to go somewhere else, don't you?"

"No. It's fine here."

She was hugging herself and it seemed to her that this annoyed him. She wore slacks and a heavy-knit sweater but she was still quite cold; she had never felt so chilled and exhausted and helpless in her life. Somewhere in Daytona Beach, in the dark, on New Year's Eve, a motel room that stank of disinfectant—she realized, now, what the odor was—a young man who stared at her without recognition, without sympathy. She had made a mistake to come to this room with him, she knew; he was going to hurt her badly.

She heard herself laughing.

"Really, it's fine! It's fine," she said, laughing. Then she began coughing. She coughed for a while, one hand pressed flat against her mouth as if she were ashamed of herself. What was so amusing? Stanley stared at her in disgust.

"Well," he said slowly, 'do you want to stay, then? Will the room be satisfactory for you?"

"Yes."

"You want me to check in?"

"Oh yes. Yes."

Still he hesitated. He pointed out a burn mark on one of the bedspreads, near the headboard. He sniffed the air; he stopped to look under the bed.

Brigit laughed, seeing him in so awkward a posture.

"Yes," he said, coloring, "it's all right for you to stand there judging me. You really don't give a damn, do you, if our honeymoon is ruined? Since we crossed the border into Florida you've been acting strangely—every five minutes you've made a comment about the weather."

"I don't believe that," Brigit said. "Surely not every five minutes—"

"What do you expect, Brigit, on New Year's Eve? On December thirty-first? It isn't summer, you know, it gets cold here in Florida and it rains occasionally, you seem to have had unrealistic expectations about the trip and now you're becoming hysterical, and we haven't unpacked and we haven't eaten dinner and I'm exhausted, I can't see straight, I'm not going to another motel no matter what you think of this one—*I'm not driving that car another mile!*"

"Yes," Brigit said softly. "I know. That's fine. I understand."

But he continued to talk: bullying, whining, accusing. She could not follow the logic of his argument. She sat suddenly on the edge of the bed, the lower part of her face frozen, locked into a foolish gay-girlish smile, a young bride's smile, and while her husband paced about the room opening and closing bureau drawers, opening and closing the bathroom and the closet doors, flinging his arms about, she cast her mind back, frightened, over the months before her marriage, trying to trace the events that led her here—as one might trace, with fastidious horror, the exact movements of two separate parties that came together in a violent collision—and every effort proved futile, every recollection of their meetings was unsatisfactory, for they had seemed, all along, really incompatible: she had never understood Stanley Fifield's innuendoes and she had often disapproved of his more explicit beliefs, but all uncertainties had been more or less swept aside by the fact that she had, evidently, "fallen in love with him" and—more importantly, perhaps—he had "fallen in love with her." And so they were married, and so he was pacing about this stucco motel room, coming closer and closer to the moment at which he would seize her shoulders and shake her violently, maddened by her limp silence, and throw her back onto the frayed bedspread.

"Now—do you love me," he would cry, "do you? Do you feel me, Brigit? *Do you feel me?*"

* * *